D'Arcy Wentworth Thompson

Day Dreams of a Schoolmaster

D'Arcy Wentworth Thompson

Day Dreams of a Schoolmaster

ISBN/EAN: 9783337402341

Printed in Europe, USA, Canada, Australia, Japan

Cover: Foto ©Andreas Hilbeck / pixelio.de

More available books at **www.hansebooks.com**

DAY DREAMS

OF A SCHOOLMASTER

BY

D'ARCY W. THOMPSON

Οὐκ ὄναρ, ἀλλ' ὄνειαρ.

BOSTON, U.S.A.

D. C. HEATH & CO., PUBLISHERS

1898

CONTENTS.

I.

THE UNDER FORM AT ST. EDWARD'S, AND THE THEORY OF ELEMENTARY UNINTELLIGIBILITY.

THIS day—October 10th, 1863—my Junior Class, in the Schola Nova of Dunedin, had its first lesson in Greek; put aside its frock and linen pants, and donned its breeches, intellectually. No transition-state is agreeable to the subject, or graceful in the eyes of a looker-on. These little fellows will all waddle, duck-like, for a considerable period in their new clothes: some will never habituate themselves thereto; but will by and by discard them, and return to the frock and linen pants; affording, it may be, a passing laugh to the unphilosophic bystander, but themselves deriving permanent comfort and unrestricted swing of limb.

The step these innocents take to-day is, of course, a step into the dark. Will the darkness, into which they so confidingly plunge, be to them perpetual and Cimmerian? or, will it duly break into a clear, bright dawn? Within three years, the majority of them will have probably passed from within these walls. What an opportunity is meanwhile afforded of wreaking upon their little heads summary vengeance for the wrongs done me by a past generation! of doing to them as I was done by! Not only should I thus be giving vent to my indignation for past ill-usage; but, strange to say, I should actually be carrying out the wishes of the parents of my victims; for, in general, those parents dread new-fangled ways; and cling piously to old scholastic superstitions. Well: for three years, then, let me lead this little flock, blind-folded, by curiously sinuous and zigzag ways; so that, always in motion, they may never progress; and at the close of the triennium, remove the bandage from their eyes, and show them, to their wonderment, that they are standing by the starting-post; that they have been dancing their Greek hornpipe on a plate.

This first lesson has turned back the dial-hand of my days, and for a passing hour I am standing in the dawn of my own most dreary, weary boyhood.

I was not quite seven and a half years old, when my dear Mother was presented with a free admission for myself, her eldest son, to the Grammar School of St. Edward. The offer was too valuable an one to admit of refusal. I was accordingly prepared for admission to my new home, by having my hair somewhat closely shorn, and by being clothed in a long, blue gown, not of itself ungraceful, but opening in front so as to disclose the ridiculous spectacle of knee-breeched, yellow-stockinged legs. After some laughter at my disguise, and much weeping at my banishment, I bade good-bye to my dear Mother. We little thought at the time that school was to be my home for twelve long years.

The day after my entry into this colossal institution, a Latin grammar was placed into my hands. It was a bulky book of its

kind: considering the diminutiveness of
the new student, a portentously bulky
book. It was bulky in consequence of its
comprehensiveness. It gave all imaginable
rules, and all imaginable exceptions. It
had providentially stored within it the requisite gear for whatever casualty might be-
fall us. The syntax rules, in the edition
presented to me, were, for the first time,
rendered mercifully in English: those for
gender and quantity remained in the old
Latin; and the Latin was communicated in
a hideously discordant rhythm. Over a
space of years we went systematically
through and through that book; page after
page, chapter after chapter. It was all unintelligible; all obscure; but some spots
were wrapt in more than ordinary gloom.
Our chronic bewilderment was varied from
time to time by shooting pains, brought on
by some passage or expression unusually
indigestible. We read of creatures, happily
few in number, that went about in the *Epi-
cœne Gender*. Were they fish, flesh or fowl?
Would the breed be ever extinct? Under
certain desperate circumstances, a participle

and a noun together were bound hand and
foot, and put into the *Ablative Absolute*.
What had they done, to be treated in a manner thus peremptory, unreasonable, crotch-
ety? Did they ever get out after being
once put in? Then there were gerunds in
Di, *Do*, and *Dum*. How they recalled to us
that old *Fee*, *Fi*, *Fo*, *Fum*, and the smell of
English blood! And supines in *Um* and *U*.
What was the meaning of these cabalistic
names? I did not know then; and I do
not know now. And yet I have been behind the scholastic curtain for twelve long
years.

There was no entire chapter in the book
more broken with pitfalls than that, composed in doggrel, which treated of the rules
for gender. Not one word, I am sure, of an
exceptionable kind had escaped the dia-
bolic ken of the compiler. String upon
string of jangling, unmusical lines could we
repeat with a singular rapidity; understanding nothing; asking no questions. Oh
the sweet, simple faith of childhood! We
had been told to commit those lines to memory, and we committed them. They would,

doubtless, do us good in the latter days. We should, at all events, be flogged there and then, unless we sang them like caged birds. It was the will of Allah: Allah was good.

Many of the words in that puzzling liturgy I have never fallen in with since, though I have been a student of its dialect for twenty-seven years. Some of the words I have since discovered to be grossly indecent in their naked English meaning. Well, well: they might have all been so, without doing more harm to our morality, than they did good to our understandings. I can vividly recollect one circumstance, that broke in a startling manner to me the dull monotony of these years. It was a hot and sultry afternoon. My wits were wandering: I suppose in green fields. So, in class-time when my turn came round, my brain was a *tabula rasa:* the inscription was clean wiped out, that had been carefully written there but half an hour before. The Master, a clergyman, had broken his cane upon a previous delinquent; his riding-whip was sent for, and I received ten lashes on my two hands. I was then under nine years of age. For a passing bewilderment, I was treated as though I had broken into an orchard. Our Master was shortly after, if I mistake not, presented to a vicarage : he was in appearance almost effeminately genteel; in dress, scrupulously neat; with fingers tapering and delicate as a lady's.

The round-shot of a Latin grammar had been, I believe, tied to our legs, to prevent our intellectually straying. However, in course of time we became habituated to the encumbrance, and ceased to feel it as a serious check upon our movements. The hour at length arrived, in which it was considered wise to attach another round-shot to our other legs. This was done accordingly in the shape of a Greek grammar, written entirely in Latin. This extra weight answered the purpose effectually : we were all brought to an immediate standstill.

I have sometimes thought, in a charitable mood, that the compiler of this book — Heaven forgive him! to word it mildly — composed it originally for such students as might be familiar with the tongue in which it was written. My comrades and I were not in that condition. We had to grapple with the difficulties of one unknown tongue through the medium of another tongue almost equally unknown. We were, in fact, required to give a determinate solution to an indeterminable problem. We had set us the equation —

$$x + y = 0;$$

and were called upon to give the values of x and y in terms of constants to be manufactured by ourselves. It was the old, old story. Bricks without straw. "Ye are idle:" said the taskmasters. So they took away our scanty wisps; but diminished nought of the tale of bricks as heretofore.

I have heard the system casuistically defended by men who, old prejudices apart, were intelligent and sagacious. "The abstract rules of grammar," said they, "are at first above the comprehension of all children. Even if they be worded in the mothertongue, it will be long before their true and full significance is apprehended. If, then, these rules be communicated in a strange language, the very difficulty surmounted in committing them to memory will imprint them the more lastingly on their understandings."

Now it would occur to me — but my simplicity may be to blame — that, if subjects, concrete or abstract, be beyond a boy's comprehension, the less he has to do with them the better. We never ask an errand-boy to *carry* a weight we know he cannot *lift*. Might not the communication of such subjects be deferred to a period, when, by a process of training, a boy's intellect were rendered capable of grasping them? Or, again, at the expense of a little time and trouble, might not the majority of grammatical rules be so simply worded, and so familiarly illustrated, as to be brought home to the intelligence of boys of ordinary capacity? I grant the difficulty, if we persist in using unintelligible terms, as *Gerunds*, *Supines*, *Aorists*, and the like; and rules that would be awkwardly enough worded, even if they were correct in substance.

But, for the sake of argument, let us admit the defence put forward for the old sys-

tem of Elementary Unintelligibility. Then, surely, we may push it to its logical issues. All will allow morality to be higher than grammar. It is, consequently, a more important task to imprint upon the minds of our children the rules of the former than the rules of the latter. But what will serve to imprint indelibly the rules of one science, will serve also to imprint the rules of another; supposing that, for the time, it be unnecessary that either set of rules be understood. Then why not communicate the Ten Commandments through the medium of Chinese? Or, if that method be found insufficiently irksome and tedious, why not improve upon the method, by rendering it physically painful? Might we not inculcate each portion of the Decalogue with the aid of a pin, and imprint it upon the memory of childhood by associating it with pricks upon some sensitive portion of the frame? In this simple manner, we might literally fasten a whole system of ethics and grammar upon the bodies as well as the brains of our little ones. The system might be extended to our university course; and a petty domestic instrument might prove a weapon of power in the hands of an energetic professor of chemistry, logic, or metaphysics! Our academic youth would go out into the world, tattooed with the records of their education. A man's own skin — and sometimes even that would be of the old material — would be his portable diploma. In two generations, not a gentleman would sit down to dinner without resting securely upon a cluster of anchors, binding him invisibly to correctness of living, reasoning, and grammar.

But to return to our Greek grammar written in Latin. Day after day our clerical Sphinx propounded the mysterious enigma. *When is a door not a door?* was the simple conundrum that confounded us. It was set us in the language of the Cumæan Sibyl, and the solution was to be given in that of the Pythian Apollo. Day after day a victim fell;

αἰεὶ δὲ πυραὶ νεκύων καίοντο θαμειαί.

When I escaped from Thebes, no Œdipus had appeared. I wonder if the Sphinx is at the old work still.

For five years — and five years make a
hole in one's school-time, not to say in one's
life — for five dreary years the process went
on. We committed daily to memory some
page or half-page of the sacred but unintelligible book. We revised it, and we
re-revised it again and again. To lisp its
contents seemed as natural as respiration.
We could repeat glibly most perplexing
declensions and conjugations; contracts of
all kinds; changes Attic, Ionic, and Æolic;
verbs in ω and verbs in μι; rules of syntax,
prosody, and construction, which no one
seemed called upon to understand at the
time, and to which, in their Latin form, no
one was, to my knowledge, ever referred
afterwards.

So far did Greek accommodate itself to
ordinary views, that we occasionally caught
glimpses of such familiar friends as *nouns*,
and *verbs*, and *prepositions*, and the like.
But here the condescension ceased. Ever
and anon came looming through the Latin
fog strange forms, gigantic, spectral; Heter-
oclites, Paradigms, Asynartetuses, Syzy-
gies; Augments, temporal and syllabic.

The former seemed to embody some dim records of a pre-Adamite state; mystic allusions to bygone Mammoths, Behemoths, Ichthyosauri; under the latter twain seemed to lurk an allegory of the connexion between Church and State.

It is a grand thing to be conversant with a noble language, unknown to all around us, to our nearest kin. It conveys an undefined idea of wealth and power. We travel where they cannot travel. We visit at great houses, and leave them standing at the door. We stand in sunlight on the hill-top, while they are groping in the valley. We wield with ease a mighty flail of thought, which they cannot uplift with both hands. Yes: we may reasonably be proud of the capability of speaking, maybe of thinking in a foreign tongue. But it is either superlatively sublime, or superlatively ridiculous, to speak for years a language unintelligible to one's-self.

But before quitting for ever the old Under Form, let me say that my quarrel has been with a system and not with persons. The only unfeeling man, under whom I had been placed, was the genteel clergyman of the

riding-whip. My other Masters were good
and kindly men, who went according to order through a dull routine, believing in it
most probably, and quite powerless from
their position, if not also from their abilities, to modify it to any material extent.
One of them, before passing further, I must
specially recall. He was the only classical
Usher; the only classical authority not in
orders; a tall, gigantically tall and muscular
Scotchman, of the name of Ramsay. *He was,
also, the only classical teacher without a cane.*
He used a strap; *Scoticè*, the tawse. Was
it because he was only an usher and a layman? or was it a kindly record of his own
more merciful training in his dear native
land? Good soul: even in the using of this
innocuous instrument, he kept his elbow on
the desk, to spare us the full sweep of his
tremendous arm. There was a silly legend
current among us, founded only on his
physical strength, that the cane had been
denied him, after his having once cut unin-
tentionally through a boy's hand, — an idle
myth, that wrapped a possibility in specious
falsehood. To see the huge *torso* towering

above the comparatively puny desk, it was like the figure-head of a man-of-war. Why, with a cane the man could have hewn a beadle to the chine, and with a birch have minced us mannikins to collops. I wonder if he had an ancestor at Bannockburn: such an one, I could imagine, with a great two-handed sword, would have chopped off English heads like turnips. I have an indistinct idea of there having been something very soft and tender in the domestic relations of that biggest and best of ushers.

But, farewell! good, kindly Usher! and farewell! good gentlemen of the Under Form!—ye deserved a better fate than the fate of Sisyphus Æolides.

II.

THE UPPER FORM AT ST. EDWARD'S AND ITS LATIN VERSES.

THE upper form consisted of three classes — the Hellenists, or House of Lords; the Deputy-Hellenists, or House of Commons; and the Erasmus, or town-council, or parish vestry, or patricio-plebeio-non-descript. Those who attained to the second rank generally stayed a year beyond the usual term: four were chosen annually from the second rank for the first; and these favorites of Fortune remained for three years on the Hellenist class, and then left for one of the Universities, with a valuable Exhibition.

The work of the Erasmus was about as tedious and unrefreshing as the old drudgery of the Under Form. That of the Deputies, to which but very few attained, became, as regards the Classics, a very little less tedious by very slow degrees; but was wholesomely vivified by the introduction of mathematical studies. How delicious, I remember, were the first lessons in geometry and algebra! they were as draughts of spring-water to lips dry with heat and chapped with sand.

Latin versification began in the Erasmus, was imperative on all, and was continued through the senior classes, whether a pupil's bent of mind were for language or science, for verse or prose. To a very few — in which minority, perhaps, I was myself included — it was an amusement, and would have been prosecuted with pleasure, had its study been optional. We members of the minority had each our special beat; our Crusoe-island, where we reigned unapproached and unapproachable. One would write hexameters, unirradiated by fancy, unblemished by flaw of rhythm or diction; another would compress epigrams, not devoid of wit, within the narrow limits of the elegiac couplet; another would attempt a comic flight, with a somewhat square-toed jocosity; another, with the false taste of enthusiastic youth, would slight the severest models of Latin verse, and spread the ideas of Keats and

Shelley over quires of dropsical hexameters
and flatulent alcaics. For myself, I would
push on patiently through the brakes of
Statius and Silius Italicus, to catch one
quaintly-dappled epithet. Many a peach-
skinned apple, somewhat flavorless to the
taste, would I steal from the hot-houses of
Claudian. I had a stock of preludes, similes,
and perorations stored away in the pigeon-
holes of my brain. Unlike the simple an-
cients, my forte lay in landscape. I had
an extensive assortment of sleeping lakes
that mirrored heaven, the emblems of quiet
souls; of winds, that rustled over peaceful
seas; of suns that went down with difficulty through washes of superfluous paint.
One sunset I have by me still. It is so gor-
geously out of all simple and severe taste,
that, could I forget my own handiwork, I
should attribute it to the pencil of a Rus-
kin. As the prelude to an ode on *Lucretia*,
it gained me a prize in books at school;
as the prelude to an ode on *The Moors in
Spain*, it gained me a gold medal at Cambridge. I could with ease adapt it, if required, for a peroration to an ode on the
Exhibition of all Nations.

But to return to my prose comrades, who formed an overwhelming majority. Latin versifying was to them a bugbear more appalling than any yet encountered. How tough-grained soever might be their idiosyncrasies of intellect — and, in many cases, the grain was very tough indeed — the wood was tapped for the regular supply of sap. Great importance was attached to the subject; and still is at all great English schools. I have not the remotest idea why. When we meet with a very odd reading in a Greek play, we presume it is correct, because any copyist would have given a reading more obvious and intelligible. So when we come upon a study of an apparently impracticable and ludicrous kind, we should hesitate before we condemn it utterly. It is plain that no ordinary brain could have suggested it. It would never have grown up of itself. If it flourish in despite of common sense, there must be a hidden sense that feeds its roots with moisture. There is, doubtless, some unseen power that troubles into usefulness the dull water of *As in præsenti;* a nymph that rises to the music of a well-turned hexameter, and re-dissolves before the discord of a false quantity. We are catholic in our views of education. There shall be no invidious distinction made between the poor and rich in brain. All our boys shall hammer at the hexameter, as all our girls are kept strumming at the piano. Shall Rugby be denied a mystery, that is allowed to every seminary of young ladies? If the theory of Latin versification be inexplicable to woman, what male intelligence could solve the riddle of those globes, whose use is esoterically taught at the humblest of our boarding-schools?

Our apprenticeship to the Latin muses lasted for about two years. Your kitten may reach his full intellectual powers in a few months; but it takes time to form an elephant or a poet. I subjoin a few sets of quasi-arranged lines. We had probably transferred to Latin verse some thousands of similar sets, before we spread our wings for original flights.

THE HORSE.

The fiery steed, his tail in air proudly cock'd,
Not without much neighing traverses glad pastures.

ALEXANDER THE GREAT.

To thee, O Alexander—learn, O ye kings, being ad-
monished—
Glory having been attained, Bacchus was a sad end.

The bee from various flowers sips sweetest honey ;
Speckled as to little body and yellow as to double
legs :
We, too, gather honey on Parnassus, a boyish crowd.
Yellow as to legs and cærulean as to flowing robe.

When duly prepared for more adventurous effort, we were set to practise upon all
the heroes and sages of antiquity ; upon
all seasons ; upon diverse accidents of fire
and flood ; and the Gradus was our Heli-
con. *Magnanimus* would help Phaëthon
on his hexametrical ride : Alexander was
practicable with a preliminary *fortis :* Hercules would have been an unmetrical brute,
but for his *alias* of Amphitryoniades, that
pushed out like a promontory half way
across the page.

A Latin couplet might be exchanged for
English verse. But it is not often that
we took advantage of the permission. The
fact is, we had no English Gradus. Our
subject one day was *Latro,* or "The Robber."
I composed my own couplet in Latin, and

furnished a friend with the following English equivalent : —

> The wicked, lurking robber, when
> The harmless traveller passes his den ;
> He seizes him by the tail of his coat,
> And robs his money and cuts his throat.

I remember also a pair of verses on the subjects, *Patroclus* and *The Last Judgment*, given in, without the least idea of joking, by a contemporary. The first ran : —

> Let us mourn, let us mourn, let us mourn for our
>   friend ;
> Let us mourn for our friend and protector ;
> Let us mourn, let us mourn, for Patroclus is dead ;
> He is kill'd by the man-slaying Hector.

And the second : —

> What can the righteous man expect,
> But to go up to heaven erect ?
> What can the wicked man desire,
> But to go down to hell-fire ?

These latter verses were not achieved by a novice. The author had been for years a nursling of the Muses ; and his English song was but an echo of the music of his Latin brother-minstrels. *Caw, Caw,* was all these honest rooks could say. And you might have whistled till you were black in the face before you would have removed

the black out of their rook-faces, or the *caw*
out of their husky throats.

In the Hellenic class we advanced to
ambitious efforts, epic and lyrical. We all
sang; some bass; some tenor; some, Heaven
only knows how. One or two of us were
very prolific. I plead guilty to having been
the juvenile parent of some two thousand
Hexameters, and of innumerable Alcaics. I
shall plead extenuating circumstances, when
I am brought before Rhadamanthus.

Many of my brother Hellenists have nothing to fear from that stern judge. They
suffered enough for their misdoings in the
actual doing. They were delivered of their
poetry with throes that cannot be uttered.
I remember the case of one Hellenist in
particular. *Il était de feu pour l'algèbre,
mais de glace pour le Latin.* In the three
Upper Forms he would have had in all probability six or seven years of continuous practice in versification. This would not be wholly suspended at the University. In his final
examination for honors, he translated the
first line of Tennyson's Beggar-maid thus:

"Brachia trans pectus posuit mendica puella."

Now, Reader, I am inclined to think that, before the days of Lucretius, there were very few lines of Latin verse that would throw this one into the shade. I am convinced that Tully never wrote a hexameter that could compare with it. I suppose there are few scholars that would acknowledge that there is an obvious natural want of the *je ne sais quoi* requisite for versification, indicated in the few metrical scraps interspersed in the works of the great Consul. And yet this man was one of the greatest masters of his own language that Italy ever produced. Without a prose literature to build upon, he has left enduring works of state-oratory, legal pleading, literary declamation, discursive essays, philosophical treatises, witty letters. He wielded the prose of his native tongue, as Ovid wielded the verse. It was put a quarter-staff into his hands, and he handled it like a rapier. However, with all the versatility of his genius, and his almost unapproachable dexterity of linguistic manipulation, he might have probably gone through all the exercises of *Bland*, *Arnold*, *and Company*, without ever producing a single

original line with the requisite poetic ring.
And yet an English classical master, in a
field where Cicero failed, will endeavor,
with a native obstinacy, to achieve success
with any pupil whatever, be he imaginative
or matter-of-fact, musical or timber-tuned;
ay, in a language foreign to both master
and pupil, and *never spoken* by either.
There is a courage in the effort, which de-
serves success.

He *may* achieve certain results, I acknowledge. A pupil, after years of profitless
toil, may acquire the mechanical power of
wedging together geometric blocks of deal
into the form of a hexameter. But the time
and trouble wasted on the acquisition of this
mechanical dexterity, might have carried
him over a broad field of reading in the
Classics, or a wide range of scientific study,
or through the leading authors of some modern literature. Alas! my English brethren
of the scholastic cloth, how long shall we
turn rapidly our gerundstones, in the vain
endeavor to grind sawdust into flour?

In regard to ancient traditions, scholastic
or political, Oxford is usually more Conser-

vative than Cambridge. It is not to the former that we should look for an attack upon Latin Verses, Port Wine, Trial by Jury, the Bench of Bishops, or any of the traditional institutions of our country. However, in regard to the tradition—I may say, superstition — of Latin versification, Oxford is in advance of the Sister-university; notwithstanding that she has records of excellence, in this particular line, superior to anything that Cambridge can show. For, leaving to a Merivale the pre-eminence in translating from English into Latin verse, we might search the prize-poems of Cambridge in vain to discover an original Latin poem to compare with the *Cursus Glacialis* in the *Musæ Anglicanæ*.

At Oxford, then, the ancient seat of the banished Camœnæ, a copy of Latin verses is said only then *to pay*, when the verses are far above mediocrity. At Cambridge, a graduation of marks may be obtained by verses that range from the ἔπεα πτερόεντα of a Senior Classic to the deal-wedges of the Wooden Spoon.

What a number of uselessly-turning gerundstones might be arrested in mid-revolution; what an amount of vainly-tortured sawdust might be set free for the stuffing of dolls or pincushions, if it were only understood that no amount of mere mechanism in versifying could obtain a mark at any examination in either University! Such a regulation would in no way affect those few scholars who cannot read their Greek and Latin poets without an occasional, and not irreverent, desire to imitate; but it would set free the energies of their prosier, but not less intelligent. brethren, for employment in more useful and congenial studies.

But, Reader, I fear I am jogging on unconsciously towards Utopia. Do you not see that such a regulation would imply, on the part of Public Examiners on the Cam, an exquisite appreciation of the differentialities of Verse and Prose? Ah! Reader, it were an easy task to examine our Undergraduates, but who shall **examine** our Examiners?

III.

THE HELLENISTS.

I HAVE been dubbed Hellenist. Nay, never start, Reader: I am too proud to be conceited. There: you need not stand un-covered. I am invested with the Latin Order of the Garter, and the Greek Order of the Golden Fleece. I am standing on a peak in Darien, and staring at a new Pacific, broad and blue, wherein lie happy islands. I have reached the zenith of all boyish hopes; surely, henceforth my path will slope down-wards to the grave. I am self-poised, self-centred. All pettiness of vanity is swallowed up in an absorbing contentment and pride. For three years I shall pace the old, shadowy cloisters; then for as many years shall I walk the garden of Academus; and then pass into the great world by one of two roads; and at the end of one road I can

dimly see men with gray wigs and silk
gowns; and at the end of the other, a circle of reverend Elders with white lawn
sleeves. O Phaëton, Phaëton, your head
is turning giddy!

To descend, then, from my dizzy flight.
I am in the middle of my seventeenth year.
I have had nine years of classical drilling.
All that I have as yet learnt might very
easily, indeed, have been acquired, had I
commenced in my thirteenth instead of in
my eighth year, and had the system of instruction been natural and easy instead of
being unnatural and difficult. This I state
unhesitatingly, after having twice carried a
class through the whole of a school curriculum of seven years.

Had it been my lot now to leave school, I
should have carried away a rather pleasant
remembrance of my first usher, and an affec-
tionate remembrance of but one Master,
Delille. It was only in the Hellenist class
that I came to love and venerate Rice, to
love and admire Webster. Speaking from
the light of subsequent experience, I believe
no school in the world ever had, or ever

will have, a trio of masters to surpass the
trio I here mention. Let me pause for a
moment, to portray them in few but loving
words.

Delille, our master of French, was a tall
and powerfully-built man, with a fresh and
ruddy complexion, and a manly carriage.
His temper was imperturbably good : his
sense of humor infectious. He had no vulgar instrument of punishment ; but by his
noble presence, and the unseen force of his
character, he could maintain the strictest
order in classes numbering above a hundred
pupils. He spoke our language without a
flaw of accent ; it was only by an occasional
hyper-correctness of *hither* for *here* that one
could detect the foreigner. His classes were
held out of the usual school-hours, sometimes even on half-holidays ; and for all that,
they were the pleasantest classes in the
under school. His severest mode of punish-
ing was to set a fable of La Fontaine to be
committed to memory. You were not re-
leased until it had been repeated without one
single break ; and you generally left him,
exasperated a little at the loss of play, but

laughing perforce at some grave piece of
badinage with which he had dismissed you.

I knew him afterwards as a friend, and
guest, and host. And what a companion he
was at table or over a cigar ! He was, like
his compatriots, a *bon-vivant;* and as good a
judge of wine as any member of a London
club. He had a splendid voice for declamation or singing ; was an admirable after-
dinner speaker in either French or English ;
could sing a song of Lover's with a rich Irish
brogue ; a song of Burns' with all the subtlety of its pure, sweet accent ; and roll out
a sea-song of Dibdin's like a sailor ! Had
I never esteemed him as a master, I should
have liked him as an accomplished man
of the world and a delightful companion.
With a number of University friends, I once
dined with him at his house in Ely Place. I
still remember the four kinds of Champagne
that were broached at dinner ; the Cham-
bertin that flowed freely afterwards with
the flow of wit and good-humor ; the music
in the drawing-room, and the singing from
ballad, opera, and oratorio ; the hour at
midnight in the snug library ; a fuming

bowl and irreproachable cigars ; and I remember, as my cab drove me to the Tavi-
stock, that the lamps of Holborn showed
through the window like mad and merry
dancing stars. Alas! I am writing of one
whose hand I shall never grasp again, for
cordial welcome or regretful farewell.

Of Webster I cannot speak at such length;
and happily for the best of reasons: he is
not, like his two colleagues, a memory alone.
But I shall never forget how contagious was
his zeal for work ; how impetuously chivalrous was his character; how thorough his
respect for industry ; how unmistakable
his abhorrence of shuffling and sloth. And
I remember thinking, at times, when I
looked up from a remarkably white hand
on the desk to a handsome and proud and
almost haughty face before me, that my
clerical Master should have been a courtly
Abbé, and have set in hall with prince and
gentle ladye.

And *Burney* — dear old Burney, as we
used to call our Head-master — how feeble
would be any words to describe our fond-
ness for that dear, white head ! The Doctor

was a noble type of the old-fashioned English Head-master. He had a loathing for all scientific study; was utterly ignorant of modern languages: indeed, I believe, he looked upon Delille as the only Frenchman that had ever been reclaimed from greasy cookery and sour claret to a repentant but honest appreciation of roast beef and port wine. English literature of the day to him was non-existent; his lectures smacked of the last century, with their long undulating periods, and pauses Ciceronian. He was the fellow-student rather than the master of his Hellenists. Patiently would he pore over their exercises, in the lighted study that sent a melancholy gleam into the long, dark school-room. All information, historical, antiquarian, geographical, or philosophic, as connected with the classics, he regarded with contempt: any dunderhead, he considered, might cram that at his leisure: but it pained him to the quick if a senior pupil violated the Porsonian pause, or trifled with a subjunctive. "A word in your ear, Doctor," said an Oxford examiner once to him; "your Captain yesterday could

not tell me where Elis was!" "I looked horrified," said the Doctor, in repeating the circumstance; "I looked horrified, of course;
but, on my word, I did not know it myself.
But," continued he, "these Oxford fellows
like this kind of thing; but I'll wager you'd
get few of them to write a good Porson."

Like all simple and unworldly natures,
he was generous to a fault. He would have
given anything, forgiven anything to a good
Greek scholar. The boys of the Under
School feared him as a strict and resolute
and severe disciplinarian. We, his Hellenists, knew that, while he followed, unques-
tioningly, old Draconian laws, his heart was
of the kindest and softest and tenderest.
How the old man, that could look so stern
at times, would weep, when an old pupil
went wrong at college; with what unre-
proaching kindness he would help him out
of difficulties, into which idleness or extrav-
agance or misfortune might have plunged
him. How like a father he would welcome
him, when all errors had been retrieved by
the winning of an honorable place in the
list of final honors. "You must remember,

Sir, that my place is due to you ; that but for your help last summer, I could not have returned for long-vacation reading." " Nonsense," replied the Doctor; " I remember nothing of the kind ; but I'll remember long enough the place you held in the classical Tripos."

And he, to whom he thus spoke, and I, who am now writing, and all who had the honor of belonging to the class of his Hellenists, will remember him with love and gratitude and reverence to the end ; ay, to the end.

And now, Reader, why should I give a description of the Hellenist class ? With three such Masters, and a set of comrades most of whom were enthusiastic students, and all of whom were pleasant fellows, how could a triennium fail to be an industrious and a happy one? — It was the reign of Antoninus Pius in my school-life, and needs no chronicling.

IV.

THE οἱ πολλοὶ, OR THE CREW OF ULYSSES.

YES, Reader, I am Hellenist. I am at the end of my third volume, and am going to live happy ever afterwards. I have reached Ithaca. A little tired and battered. But I have reached Ithaca. I will now take mine ease by my own hearth, and spin long yarns about Scylla and Charybdis. But where are my old comrades? Poor fellows! they are all drowned. They are lying at the bottom of that Ægean, which in life was the scene of all their suffering, and the reservoir of all their geography.

The fact is, it was only in exceptional cases, that boys with us remained at school after the age of fifteen. Consequently, my old friends were all away. They had gone for the most part into commercial life. Fortunately, one-half of their schooling had been devoted to the despised branches of

penmanship, ciphering, reading, and writing
from dictation. These subjects had been
very well taught. Indeed, had they been
. taught ever so indifferently, the pupils
could scarcely have failed to pick up something in such elementary branches during a
curriculum of at least seven years. Consequently, in the various counting-houses
into which they were draughted, our boys
were usually found good penmen, ready
reckoners, and tolerably correct in their
spelling. But of one entire half of their long
school probation, the majority carried away
no intellectual memento. Upon that half
had been brought to bear the most expensive part of the educational machinery;
masters of arts instead of ushers; clergy-
men instead of laymen; dictionaries and
lexicons instead of copy books and slates.
There had been no lack of sowing; but there
had been no reaping; no gathering into
barns: although, Heaven knows! the ground
had been well harrowed, and the seed had
been watered plentifully, and with tears.

I must state in passing, that there was a
naval school into which boys might enter,

at their own option, about the age of twelve.
Many, that had no special calling for a sail-
or's life, entered it with the mere view of
escaping a life of Latin and Greek drudgery on dry land.   This part of the school
had been added to the original foundation
by Charles II. Every year a little deputation
presents at Court its charts and drawings,
in accordance with the expressed wish of
the royal founder. I believe in no portion of
the kingdom is a course of naval instruction
given so perfect in both practice and theory.

My contemporaries of the ordinary Under
Form, who survive, will be now in the prime
of manhood. Do they ever look calmly back
upon the miraculous fog, that overhung one
half of their seven years' schooling ? Have
they ever expiscated one intelligible reason
why they were so long detained in the barren wilderness ? What good have they ever
reaped themselves from the trial; or, what
gratification can it have afforded to others?
Or, seems that period to them an embryo-
state; a dream within a dream? Some of
them will now be Benedicks; some will have
boys growing into their teens. Our species,

like the sheep, is prone to follow a lead. I
would venture to affirm, that these fathers
will, in most instances, be putting their
boys through some similarly mysterious
educational process.

The fact is, men usually look back upon
their school days, as a pedestrian upon
traversed, far-off, blue hills. *He* forgets the
long, desolate moorlands ; the tortuous path-
ways ; the morasses here and the shingles
there ; the peak on peak, that never was
the highest. *They* forgive, over the walnuts
and the wine, the pedagogue that thrashed
them to no moral or mental profit; the
bully, that appropriated their weekly sixpence ; the old house-keeper, that worried
them with nig-nagging for their torn linen,
or for faces dirtier than their dirty shoes.
School was not such a bad place after all.
Another glass or two of the old, tawny particular; and, faith! we were never so happy
as in our boyhood, and may never be as
happy again. Besides, boys are terribly in
the way at home; and school is the real
place for them after all; and, depend upon
it, if there were no virtue in birching, caning,

Latin verses and Greek what-ye-may-call-'ems, they would not have held their ground so long amongst a practical people like ourselves. So Johnny is sent to the Town Grammar School, and returns in due time with as much honey of Hymettus on his legs, as his father before him. And meanwhile, the great, time-honored Gerundstone turns, and will turn to the last syllable of recorded time.

In the majority of great English Public Schools, the primary subjects of writing, ciphering, reading and spelling, are notoriously ill taught. The chief modern languages, French and German, languish in the cold shade of their classic rivals. And yet, elementarily, they are taught on a more rational plan than the Classics. That is to say, the rules of nature or common sense are not wholly ignored; and the conversational, *vivâ voce* principle is to some extent kept in view. But success in these departments carries with it no acknowledged prestige; paves the way to no brilliant University distinction. Too frequently, also, a master of French is a master of French only, with no more claims to learning than a *chef-de-cuisine* ; and too often a master of German will mar the effect of his erudition by a philosophic but frowsy disregard of toilet proprieties. And alas! a foreigner, however learned and well-mannered, too often fails in the maintenance of discipline, from the fact that the idea of order is, to his pupils, inseparably connected with a vigorous use of implements, which are barbarous in his eyes and ridiculous in his hands.

However, be the condition of other branches what you please, the melancholy fact stands, that the Classics are taught in such a way as to benefit only those who, by superior talents or inordinately long continuance at school, eventually emerge from the darkness overhanging their elementary training. I could enumerate three historical and well-endowed metropolitan schools, to which, in my day, even this latter exceptional statement was not due.

In the Under School at St. Edward's, we certainly understood the husbandry of making a very little Greek go a very long way. We sank our teaching plummet many

fathoms deep in the abyss of Unintelligibility. But the historical trio had tumbled
through the antipodes to the nadir, where
they were sticking like rayless stars. There
were honey-prizes, in the way of Exhibi-
tions and Scholarships attached to these
drone-hives: they must have been assigned
to such drones as were found pre-eminent
in weight or size or capacity of repose.

At the best of the great Public Schools,
the youngest children—bless the innocents!
—are suckled upon grammar; the more
advanced are too often fed upon dull books,
made duller by superfluous annotations; the
manuals for prose composition are in many
cases tramways to pedantry exhibiting for
imitation the unintentional faults of Thucy-
dides and the intentional faults of Tacitus;
the manuals for Latin versification would
seem to have been originally intended to
implant in boys a quick perception of the
ludicrous. A vile system of *literal transla-
tion* of Greek and Latin idioms so corrupts
the well of English undefiled, that a boy
often loses as much English in his Latin
room, as he will pick up for the day in his

English one. No one, after once the sentences have been analyzed, would ever dream
of translating literally *Comment vous portez
vous ?* or, *Qu'est-ce que c'est que ça ?* but pedantry will insist upon boys rendering, year
after year, Greek particles by the most un-
English equivalents, and Latin redundancies
by English wind. The whole system, and
the elementary part most of all, is bookish,
unpractical. It is many years — nay, very
often it does not happen at all, — it is many
years, at all events, before a lad suspects
that Latin and Greek are instruments of
thought precisely similar to his own everyday language. In the earlier years of his
apprenticehood, he would almost scout the
idea as profane, that men could under any
circumstances exchange chit-chat; write
love-letters; deliver after-dinner speeches;
tell Joe Millers; make bad puns in such solemn and stiff-jointed forms of speech. *Indeed, they never strike him as forms of speech
at all.* He may entertain a hazy idea that
Latin was employed by a Roman tradesman
for composing an Elegiac valentine, or an
advertisement in Alcaics. Its grammatical

nomenclature is worded differently from
that of any modern tongue; and that for
Greek is worded more cabalistically still.
He meets with no Aorists in English; no
Supines in French; no Gerunds in German;
no Paulo-post-futures anywhere in the habitable world.   And yet I will venture to
say, that there are very few idioms of either
Greek or Latin that have not their analogues
in homely Saxon and pure French.   Indeed,
I am almost inclined to think that the use
of ἄν in Greek is the only idiom to which it
would be difficult or impossible to adduce a
parallel.   Why on earth, then, are the former
pair swathed in a verbiage so peculiar?   I
can understand the use of a peculiar nomenclature in days when the theory of language
was imperfectly understood; and I freely
acknowledge the debt of gratitude due to
the old grammarians for raising the struc-
ture before us, with the scanty materials at
their disposal.   Latin was then considered as
radically different from Greek, as Greek,
from Coptic.   Ay, and might be considered so
now, for all the teaching in our schools.   The
magnificent, cloud-dispelling   discoveries

of Bopp and the Grimms, so full of interest
if *gradually* and clearly expounded, to
young and old alike, are in most class-rooms
practically ignored. We still separate by
arbitrary boundaries studies that we know,
or should know, to be cognate. If Latin,
Greek, and Teutonic are really sisters, and
French a daughter of one of them, why
should it be thought impossible to teach
them all upon some catholic plan? At the
very least, the grammatical terms employed
in one school-room might be employed in
another. Take, for instance, such a simple
sentence as, *I should like to know.* If a boy
were called upon to parse such a sentence
in three consecutive class-rooms, he would
find a Conditional mood in the French
room, a Subjunctive one in the Latin, and
an Optative one in the Greek. A very Proteus of a mood; now a bear; now crack-
ling fire; now running water, that slips
through one's fingers.

I am convinced in my own mind that it
were practicable to teach English, French,
German, Latin, and Greek on a broad and
catholic system. The first step would be

for the patrons of our great schools to require of every candidate for a classical mastership satisfactory proofs of a thorough
knowledge of French or German, or even of
both languages, in grammar and *accent*. If
a good classical scholar were found deficient
in the latter particular, he might be advised
to travel abroad, to cure his ear and his
tongue of their insular vulgarity. In a few
years, a scholar would as soon think of
speaking French with a bad accent as of
eating peas with a knife. A class might
pass from language to language, *retaining
its shape and the position of its members ;*
upon the principle that it was merely passing
from one to another phase of one great and
comprehensive subject. Thus, the places in
a class of English, French, or German, would
be thrown in with those of Latin and Greek
at the end of a session, to determine the prizes
for proficiency in the broad and catholic
study of the dialects of one common language. The classics would benefit by the
amalgamation, as they would have to be
treated less mysteriously, and illustrated
more interestingly ; and to modern lan-

guages would be given a prestige in the eyes of the pupils, which they have hitherto most unquestionably and most undeservedly lacked.

To some the amalgamation proposed may seem one of incongruities. It is not so. It is much more incongruous to mix the study of modern history with the study of Latin and Greek, than to associate the study of one language with that of another cognate language, in the determination of class places. A boy may have a special turn for history and the acquisition of general information, who is comparatively slow at linguistic studies. But a good scholar in Latin and Greek will be a good scholar in French and German — *if he choose.* I have known lamentable instances of good classical scholars neglecting purposely, and for sordid reasons connected with school prizes, the study of modern languages; but I could also point to separate class-lists where the same names, almost in the same order stood as prizemen in four languages, ancient and modern; and this would be found generally the case, if some such system as the one suggested were adopted.

With such a system in operation, the pedantic phraseology of our classic manuals would have to be modified, of course; the examples to the majority of rules to be pitched in a lower and more natural key. We have, at present, a genteel and superstitious dread not only of solecisms, but of commonness in expression; forgetting, most unphilosophically, that the vulgar tongue is in all cases the real tongue; that where we can hear a language in its pure, unadulterated vulgarity, — and any one but a Bagman knows the term is not necessarily synonymous with coarseness or slang, — there have we in Italy a correcter language than the polished diction of Ovid; and in England more home-spun stuff that can be drawn from Pope and Gray. Such a line, for instance, as —

Cujus ebur nitidum *fastigia* summa tegebat,

might be justified in Ovid, on the score of difficulty in adapting his language to a foreign metre; but the collocation of the words is obviously wrong either for Latin or for any language. Again, such a line as —

Utendum est *ætate;* cito pede præterit ætas,

is exquisitely worded. But the former part of the line is only right according to the rules of fashionable grammar, or that of analogy and imitation, and wrong according to the rules of *real* grammar. The poet's valet would never have committed the blunder; he would never have assigned to the active *utendum* the government of the reflective *uti*. He would no more have thought of attaching an abnormal case to an ordinary verb, than of pinning a verb to his tunic.

In our servile admiration of what is falsely called purest Latin, our hankering after Augustan elegancies, we lose sight of the homely, conversational treasures that, might be extracted copiously from Plautus, less copiously from Terence, and to some extent, if we taught Latin as we ought to teach it, from our own brains. If, by the adoption of a *vivâ voce* conversational method in elementary classes, a pupil once got a natural, unconscious grip of Latin, style and polish would follow easily enough, as the method gradually became more searching, critical, and analytic. In our own language, we never illustrate early les

sons by elaborately poised sentences from
Robertson or Gibbon; but with random
speech; familiar instances; common saws.
We wait patiently until the pupil gets a
tight hold of his subject, before we call upon
him to wield it with rhetorical effect. A
round single-stick suffices for the first rude
lessons in the use of the trenchant broad-
sword. So in the illustration of the rules
of Latin Syntax, I would advocate the use
of familiar everyday sentences, such as a
boy might carry about with him as unconsciously as he does his jacket. I should not
be afraid to employ many a word that might
be searched for in vain in the pages of Cicero, or even in the dull pages of a dictionary; to let pass uncorrected many a phrase
that would send a shudder through an Augustan precisian. In fact, I should treat
Latin and Greek as though I were not in
the least afraid of them; as though there
were no special linguistic secrets wrapped
within their mantles; as though they were
simple, honest, straight-forward languages,
like the one spoken without conscious effort by our own street ragamuffins.

So far, however, from ignoring the value of style and finish, I should merely be deferring their inculcation until I could inculcate them with effect. It seems labor thrown away to demonstrate that *this* is more elegant than *that*, when *this* and *that* are both imperfectly understood.

Again: at present, ere a boy by the glimmering light of a misty dictionary, or the reflected light of his solar tutor, can grope through the involutions of an ordinary paragraph, he is pushed into works that would probably little interest him, could they be perused as easily as his own Robinson Crusoe. Cornelius Nepos and Sallust are two special bugbears. Cæsar is not wholly blameless. I can well imagine a scholar-like soldier or historian reading the latter with pleasure and profit. But, apart from the difficulty of frequently-recurring indirect speeches, his narrative, with all its soldierlike simplicity and directness, is too extended for boys who can only read it in detachments. We ourselves could enjoy no landscape, however beautiful, that we saw only in separate rounds through a paper tube. But who will stand bail for those other notoriously old offenders? What grown man, though reeking with Latin, would give an evening hour to the twaddle of the one, or the pedantry of the other? And what versatility of human wit could render either interesting to children in miserable, daily pittances of eight lines? which eight lines would have first to be tortured into villanous English; then parsed, word by word; the nouns all declined; the verbs all conjugated: — a ruminative process; — then, after pausing to take breath, we should begin again at the end, and reverse the order of proceeding; running backwards through the verbs, and backwards through the nouns. And so on, *ad nauseam.   O dura pueror' ilia!*

V.

ON CLIMBING.

IMAGINE yourself, Reader, in an elementary class-room, and before you a semicircle of some fifty little recruits upon the benches, with their brain-pans newly primed with the singular of *penna.* "Make ready ! — present ! ! — fire ! ! !" and pop go the fire-arms. But what a scattered volley! Some, it is true, discharge their six rounds with precision ; but some are firing off their ablatives half a minute behind their comrades, and some poor unfortunates of the awkward squad have missed fire at their genitive shot.

Follow me now, Reader, through the scenes of our ordinary Latin drama. The subject-matter of the play is a somewhat confused one : if, therefore, in the description I indulge in a Castlereagh-medley of metaphors, the fault is in the subject, and not in myself.

The singular of *penna* is our rehearsal for to-day, with that of a few similar nouns: the plural of the same will come to-morrow: on the day following the singular and plural in combination. Then in order will come *dominus* and suite; then *puer* and ditto; then *liber* and do.; and so on, until we pause with *dies* and *res.*

Then separately and in order will stalk across the stage, *bonus, bona, bonum; mitis, mite; felix;* with their three legs, and two legs, and one leg. Then come their invidious comparatives, and their bombastic superlatives. Then the pronouns; then an active verb of the first conjugation, as *amo;* then, actives of the other conjugations in order, as *moneo, rego, audio;* then the verb *sum;* then the passives in due order; then adverbs, numerals, prepositions, conjunctions.

Now I shall quit the stage, and set you down to dinner, at our *pièce de résistance,* Syntax. Thin separate slices are taken day by day without vegetables, bread, or salt; they will, consequently, remain upon the stomach; will 'cause, certainly, indigestion; will, possibly, leave a chronic irritation of the mucous membrane.

Back, Reader, to the stage. The footlights are dimmed, and the actors are groping their way through the defiles of *Propria quæ maribus*, and *As in præsenti* —

"Lasciate ogni speranza, voi, che 'ntrate."

Thus our class is taken through the pages and chapters of its grammar, with its attention riveted exclusively on its daily lesson; on its daily square-yard of Latin. It is a process somewhat analogous to that of traversing a dictionary, by stages, from A to Z. Or it may be considered as a process of stratification, applied to the administering of mental food. And yet, physically, no man would ever take his dinner in separate layers of beef and potatoes and bread; and no elderly gentleman would take his punch in separate instalments of rum and water and sugar and lemon-peel. Or again, it may be considered as a process of bolting mental food in lumps; which process, physically, is not conducive to digestion.

I acknowledge that the system, wooden as it is, produces, or fails to hinder, some good results in pupils of high intelligence after a course of four or five years' teaching; because intelligence in boyhood *will* twist through obstacles into knowledge as a branch does into sunlight; and common sense in manhood *will* at times slip off the grooves that routine may have laid down. But, with an easier and more interesting method, I assert that, after a similar period, the more intelligent might have done far more, and the less intelligent a great deal; whereas, at present, the more intelligent do very little, and the less intelligent next to nothing.

But it will be said, that there is no *regia via* to knowledge; that the latter is found only at the summit of the Hill of Difficulty; which we may never reach by walking on a level road. True: but there are more ways than one of ascending a hill; and the one which seems the shortest, is often found the longest; and he who tries it, often meets midway with some insuperable difficulty, and is forced to retrace his steps, and

recommence the ascent by an easier and less fatiguing route. Instead of breasting a steep hill, and pushing upwards in a line, gazing only at the heath or shingles at my feet, I should prefer taking long circuitous bends, to lessen the angle of ascent; and, as the labor would thus be rendered less exhaustive, I should be enabled on my way to enjoy the expanding prospect; to watch the sailing clouds above, and the valley and the lake spread underneath. In this way I have climbed Skiddaw and Benlomond without over-fatiguing myself: I tried Ben-Rattachan by the other way, unsuccessfully; and paid dearly for the attempt.

So, in the study of a language, I acknowledge that there *is* an ascent to be made; but I hold it my duty, as a guide, to point out to the pedestrians under my charge such a pathway as may present the angle of least inclination.

In the declensions and conjugations—say, of Latin — as we find them, there is so much of phonetic corruption, that the changes of termination may be, for a while at least, regarded as arbitrary. Had we them presented to us in their primitive form, memory would be little needed and judgment would do almost all our work. As it is, memory is here absolutely required. The declensions and conjugations, then, *must* be committed to memory; at first, unreasoningly; we must wait awhile, before we give the solution to the riddles of their inflexions; some, perhaps, we shall have to leave unsolved. The rules of gender also, and the commonly recurring exceptions, must be similarly learned; they may be compressed *within a page and a half* of an ordinary octavo. We may, reasonably, take it for granted that a young student of Latin is capable of analyzing an ordinary sentence in his own language: that, in the following sentences —

(1.) This is my father's hat:
(2.) He loved his brother :
(3.) He gave me nothing:
(4.) This is the house that Jack built:
(5.) There is no saying:

he will understand that

(1.) *My* is in the possessive case, as agreeing with the possessive *father's ;*

That (2.) *his brother* is an accusative or *primary object* after *loved ;*

That (3.) *nothing* is accusative after *gave ;* and *me*, dative or *secondary object ;*

That (4.) *the house* is nominative after *is,* a verb of existence ; and *that*, although referring to a nominative, itself an accusative after the active-transitive verb built ;

That (5.) *saying*, although spelt as a participle, is a verbal noun, or a noun coined out of a verb, and in reality the nominative to *is*, and only put after it for convenience, in consequence of the intrusion of the superfluous and anticipatory word, *there.*

Unless a pupil shall know thus much, and a good deal more of the grammar of his own language, it would seem to me to partake of the nature of folly or cruelty to push him into the syntax of a foreign one.

Taking for granted, then, such preliminary knowledge in our novice, the difficulties of Latin syntax are wonderfully lessened. *The great majority of its rules he is already acquainted with :* they are common to that syntax of simple rules, by which he *should daily parse, with his Latin*

Master, his paragraph of English. He will find that there are after all but very few rules of syntax in Latin, which might not be applied to his own tongue. He will, however, see that, in Latin, an adjective is not invariable in its spelling as with us; but partakes of the nature of the mocking-bird, and imitates, musically but not always usefully, its noun in gender, number, and case. He will observe, also, that with nouns, Latin expresses many things — such as the *manner, how; the means, by which; the time, when* — by case-endings, which things English usually expresses by prepositions; in other words, that Latin uses *tight affixes,* where we prefer *loose prefixes.* But he will see that English also has its tight affixes in such words as *father's, him, them, whom, loves, loveth, loving, loved.* So, even in this respect, he will see that there is a partial agreement between modern English and ancient Latin, which at first seemed so totally different. And I will now hint to him, and by and by will prove to him, that his own language had once as many tight affixes as Latin, but dropt them by

degrees; just as Latin did, as it merged into what is now called Italian.

It will very probably, then, be found that
such Latin syntax, as he may be called upon
to commit to memory, may be compressed
within *at most two pages.* The rules for
prosody should, I consider, be expunged *in
toto* from his grammar. All that is neces-
sary herein may be communicated orally by
a Master in the scansion of lines, from day
to day, when his class comes to read Ovid,
or Virgil, or Horace. Indeed, the analysis
of noun and verb terminations, carried on
from day to day, will gradually explain upon
reasonable grounds almost all abnormal
quantities. I think it would be difficult to
bring forward in Latin half a dozen *long
vowels,* final or otherwise, which could not
be explained on the principle of the blending of vowels or the softening of a consonant. I have tried this oral method twice
with two sets of upper classes, of which I
had the divided, though subordinate, charge,
and can furnish full proofs of its success.

The numerals also must be committed to
memory, and may be so committed in at

most two lessons. To learn by rote long strings of prepositions or conjunctions is to my mind worse than useless. They should be communicated orally, gradually; like kindly gifts, stealthily. Thus, upon examination, we find that all that requires unreasoning memory may be reduced to the following heads : —

(1.) The five declensions, which include all adjectives and participles :

(2.) The rules for gender, and exceptions :

(3.) The four conjugations, active and passive, which latter voice includes *sum :*

(4.) The irregular verbs, *eo, volo, nolo, malo, possum :*

(5.) Syntax; two pages.

All this might easily be comprehended within twenty-four octavo pages. It is only a hillock of difficulty. But instead of climbing right up the face of it — for the sides may be very steep, though the summit be within rifle-range — I should guide a pupil by the sinuous and not uninteresting path, along which I beg of you, Reader, to accompany me in the next chapter.

VI.

FROM PENNA TO POSSUM.

I SHALL suppose myself to have a class of about fifty little fellows seated before me, impressed with the solemnity of the occasion, and carrying each the bâton of a School-marshal in his pocket. I shall take it for granted that they have had a previous training of two years at some one or other of the excellent preparatory schools of our own Dunedin; and that this training has been wisely confined to English grammar, spelling, reading, and elementary arithmetic; and not mischievously extended to Latin rudiments for the muddling of their as yet imperfect ideas of English. I shall also suppose that they are all ten years of age, with a margin on either side.

Under these circumstances I should commence operations; and it would be my earnest endeavor from this first lesson to the last they should receive from me, to disrobe their new language little by little of its mysterious integuments, and, if possible, to prove it in the end to be composed of the same flesh and blood and bones as their own Teuton mother-tongue.

For a week or so I should content myself with probing their knowledge of English grammar; and from time to time I should draw their attention to those few inflexional terminations that our own language has still retained; as in *him, them, whom, dost, loveth* or *loves;* and I should impress upon them that it was in such words that English displayed what was the chief characteristic of Latin, viz., the use of *tight affixes* instead of *loose prefixes;* and I should repeatedly inculcate this fact, that the chief difference, if not the only difference, between the two languages, was, that *English used loose prefixes very often, and tight affixes very seldom; and that Latin used tight affixes very often, and loose prefixes as seldom as possible.* And I would illustrate this by the present tense of the verb *to love,* and that of *amare :* —

I love, ...	*Amo,*
Thou lovest, . . .	*Amas,*
He loveth or loves, .	*Amat,*
We love, . . .	*Amamus,*
Ye love, . . .	*Amatis,*
They love, . . .	*Amant ;*

and I should request them to observe that in the English tense there were four identical words love; but that in the Latin tense all the words were different; and I should then show them how requisite it was for us in English to use our *pronouns* with our verbs, to prevent mistakes; but that it was not so requisite in Latin, as the persons in both numbers were all spelt differently.

And if I met with such a sentence as, *The king sent him,* I should point out how independent we were here of the order of our words; how, without ambiguity, we might say —

Him the king sent ; or
The king him sent ;

because that the spelling of *him* plainly indicated that, *in sense,* even if not *in position,* it was to follow or be governed by the verb *sent.*

But if I came to such a sentence as, *The boy stuck the pig*, I should observe that here we were unable to alter the position of our words without imminent danger to the boy. And I should show them how much more freely in such a sentence we might have handled the pig, if he had retained his accusative in addition to his tail; how we might then have caught hold of him by his accusative, and put him anywhere in the above sentence, without his being able to do harm to the boy; and I should observe that, in Latin, pigs as well as pronouns had accusatives; and not only pigs, but nouns of all kinds, masculine and feminine — for, of course, those stupid neuter nouns could hardly expect them — and that it was only in modern times that nouns, indiscriminately, had been treated worse than terrier-puppies, and lopped into guinea-pigs and Manx cats.

And thus for a week or so, under cover of our parallels of English parsing, should we approach, gradually and warily the Sebastopol of our Latin Grammar. And, meanwhile, on one of our public days, some parents of my pupils would pay my class a visit; and one of them, perhaps, returning home, would say that he could not understand my method: which would very probably be true: and that he should remove his boy from my class at the close of the current quarter; which he would very probably do; perhaps, not to the great benefit of his boy.

At length we open our grammar and commence with *penna*. Its singular consists of six words. When these had been thoroughly committed to memory by each and every pupil, I should request them to limit their attention for the present to the three cases —

> The Nominative,
> The Genitive or Possessive, and
> The Ablative;

and I should request them to write down on their memories, or in a copy-book, if they preferred, these three cases for the following nouns —

> *puella,*   *aquila,*
> *aqua,*   *matrona,*
> *ala,*   *ancilla;*

and the same for the adjectives —

bona,	*nigra,*
mala,	*pessima,*
candida,	*optima ;*

and by means of these, and the simple word *est*, we might form scores of sentences. These sentences might be varied by placing two nouns together, as, *ala aquilæ*, or *aquilæ ala :* we might then throw in two prepositions *in* and *cum*, governing the ablative; and a pupil would thus, in one lesson, be furnished with verbal machinery for forming sentences without number; common familiar sentences, such as he might use at dinner-table or in the playground, if he chose.

In due time let us take the plural of *penna*, and that of the six similar nouns, and of the six feminine adjectives; and decline them with adjectives in combination with nouns, till each and every pupil has them at his finger-ends; and let us revise the lesson of the previous day. Now, then, let us throw in the word *sunt*, and a few adverbs of common occurrence in ordinary talk; as *nunc, tunc, semper, nunquam ;* and repeat, with our extended vocabulary, the *vivâ voce* process of the preceding day or days.

Let our next lesson be the singular and plural of *penna ;* with the singular of *dominus.* Let us now decline, like the latter, six familiar nouns; and the masculines of the adjectives before mentioned; and pause awhile to illustrate the echoing propensities of a Latin adjective: then let us throw in one or two more familiar adverbs, and proceed with our *vivâ voce* as before.

For the next day, let us be similarly engaged with the plural of *dominus* and the like nouns and adjectives; and for our *vivâ voce* throw in the masculines and feminines of the following participles —

amatus,	*fractus,*
culpatus,	*monitus,*
laudatus,	*auditus ;*

remembering that, *hitherto, in our spoken sentences, we are limited to the use of the three originally specified cases.*

When I reach *regnum*, I may throw in the neuters of all the adjectives and participles hitherto used; and, meanwhile, we may have introduced the present tense of · *sum*, and additional adverbs or adverbial expressions from time to time.

Thus, on arriving at the end of the second declension, we shall have a somewhat extensive vocabulary; and by a skilful use of it we may vary our spoken sentences almost *ad infinitum.*

By and by, the present tense of *amo* should be introduced, with that of a few similar verbs; *and we should then call in simultaneously the accusatives of all our declinable words to follow active-transitive verbs.*

The indicative mood of *sum* and *amo* might thus be introduced, by instalments, before we reached the end of the fifth declension. And meanwhile our attention would have been *confined entirely to nouns regular in inflexion and gender;* the irregulars being left to be incorporated in due time.

While the declensions were being rigorously committed to memory, we should almost imperceptibly be throwing in prep-

osition, adverb, or tense, that would enable
. the pupil to use his little store of declined
words almost as soon as he acquired it. We
should in fact have used our declensions as
the boiling water, and the extraneous words
as our oatmeal; and by scattering in the
latter gradually and in thinnest streams
and adding such *sales* as were at hand, we
should probably have provided a porridge
not wholly indigestible.

We should now proceed to our verbs.
They would now be transmuted to the
water, and the nouns to component parts
of the oatmeal. Three tenses per diem
would, probably, be our allowance; but to
every tense we should append strings of
examples, and would be gradually increasing our vocabulary of words, and using
those numerous rules of syntax, in which
Latin is in harmony with English. It would
be as well to classify our nouns, as we introduced them. One day we might attach
to one or two well-conned verbs the names
of trees or flowers; similarly, we might
make our pupils familiar with the names
of beasts and birds and fishes; the articles

of ordinary furniture in a Roman dwelling,
the parts and rigging of a ship; terms military; terms of courtesy; degrees of con-
sanguinity; not mapping out our proceedings on all occasions, but following nature
and impulse; and we should, doubtless, find
their guidance more direct than that of any
trumpery Delectus in existence.

And all the while, we should be endeav-
oring to deceive our little fellows, by con-
cealing from them the real amount of their
increasing stores. So long as we abstained
from using a pedantic and dull grammar,
we should easily deceive, in this respect, a
number of their parents, who would be
firmly persuaded that their children were
learning nothing. For in the minds of
many people, education is inseparably connected with the idea of difficulty and tediousness. They imagine that a great deal
must be accomplishing, when painful efforts are being made. They find a grim
satisfaction in the feeling of obstruction.
So when you row a boat against the stream,
you hear the water ruckling at the prow,
and you feel virtue go out of you at every

sweep of the oar; and the boat is almost stationary. But, when you row with the current, you hear no noise of rippling; you scarcely feel your oar; and the boat is gliding like a swan.

Some such method as that above — and remember, a *vivâ voce* method can, at the best, be drawn in but faintest outline upon paper — would lead boys to catch with rapidity sentences *of great length, so long as the construction were not involved.* They would almost insensibly be brought to think in Latin; that is to say, it would very soon sound as ridiculous in their ears, to put *ille* after *amo* as to put *he* after *I love;* and this *intuitive perception* of the grammar of a language, as connected with its musical sound, is one of the first requisites for a subsequent thorough knowledge of, and capacity of *easy handling* the same. And the process for acquiring this intuitive perception is not so difficult as it is usually thought to be. It is, in fact, not a very high mental process. It is acquired by postilions abroad and foreign waiters here, without great difficulty or delay. But although it is not a highly intellectual acquisition, it is a wonderfully useful one, to serve as a foundation for a really intellectual struct- ure.   And I am convinced that some such process should be employed with a novice in Latin, and in any language he may be approaching; and that it is a positive cru- elty to pin him wholly down for a year to monotonous lessons of memory, or to worry him too soon with formal rules for parsing.

VII.

FROM POSSUM TO PHÆDRUS.

THE course of study, sketched out in rough outline in the preceding chapter, would require, perhaps, a session, or at least three quarters of a sessions, for the filling in of such shading as would be requisite to make of our sketch a finished and sightly drawing. Whilst memory had been continually engaged on the road from *Penna to Possum*, we should imperceptibly have introduced all those rules of syntax wherein Latin and English — and, indeed, all the Arian languages — are at one.

We might now attack, still upon the *vivâ voce* method, those few rules, wherein the idiom of Latin is, or seems to be, at variance with that of our own tongue. We might, for a time, ingraft one such rule upon the work of each day; then ingraft them by

twos; then by threes; then illustrate their.
at random. And in all our illustrations we
should use familiar expressions, and contrast the Latin and English methods of
expressing some one idea or circumstance.
Thus, for such a sentence as, *He struck the
tree with an axe*, we might show how the use
of the Latin *cum* in such a sentence would
convey the notion of companionship; or
that he struck the tree *along with* an axe.
And in such a sentence as, *He wrote the
letters with many tears*, we might show that
to omit the *cum* in Latin would convey the
idea of *instrumentality*, or that *he wrote the
letters with tears as a sort of invisible ink*.
Such idioms we might illustrate, so familiarly and repeatedly, that their force could
scarcely fail to be appreciated by the majority of, and perhaps by all, our pupils.
And all this while, I must remind the
reader that our class is supposed *to be engaged daily, for at least one hour, in the
strict and rigorous analysis of some English
paragraph;* and that, during every such lesson in English grammar, attention is drawn
to those cases where the habits of the two

languages are at one, and where their idioms are really *or apparently* at variance.

By this time we should be prepared to take in hand some Latin book for reading. And here I should probably be compelled, not without reluctance, to commence with some Latin Delectus or Reader; but, afterwards, I should strongly object to any edition of a simple classic that should be encumbered with notes or vocabularies. I would recommend, for instance, a simple text-edition of the Fables of Phædrus: and such an edition would combine cheapness with utility : and I should take daily a fable *at random, which should be made out in my presence.* If, in such a fable, I saw a word not previously met with, or a difficult construction, or — what is not unfrequent — a piece of questionable Latinity, I should give due explanation or warning. And I should certainly never allow a fable to extend over even two days, for fear of my pupils losing interest in their work. And now I should commence systematically parsing my Latin lessons, and would draw special attention to diversities of idiom; but I would never call upon a boy to repeat pedantic and too often meaningless rules; but only to answer directly such questions as were put to him. Thus, in such a sentence as, *Suo se gladio miles vulneravit*, if I asked the gender of *suo*, I should expect him only to say *masculine;* and if I asked him to say why it were so, I should expect him to reply, that it was so in imitation of, or in agreement with the gender of *gladio*, its noun: and if I asked him the case of *suo*, I should be content with the simple reply that it was *ablative;* and if I further asked him *why*, I should expect him to explain it on the same principle of imitation or agreement: but if I asked him why *gladio* were *ablative*, I should expect him to say that it was so as expressing the *means by which* the soldier did the deed. And, perhaps, before very long I should tell him that the *ablative* case meant the *taking away* case, and I should ask him to find fault with the expression *ablative case of the instrument;* and he would doubtless perceive that *the taking away case* could hardly be *the case of means by which*, and I then should request him to say simply, when asked the case of *gladio* in such a sentence, that it was the *case of instrument*, or *of means by which.* And I should similarly point out the absurdity of such expressions, if I ever met with them, as *ablative of the cause, ablative of time, genitive of place;* and suggest that it would be no less ridiculous for us to speak of *the waking condition of sleep,* or *the active condition of repose.*

And if I came to such a sentence as *Puer librum tabulæ imposuit,* I should explain how *imposuit* meant *put on;* and I should say that if a boy *put,* he must first have *put something;* and that this something might be called the *primary object* after the transitive verb; and that if he put something *on,* he must also have put that something *on something else,* which something else I should expect to find in the case of the *secondary object:* unless a special preposition were used, as in English: and so in the above Latin sentence he would see that *librum* was the primary object depending on the *posuit* in the verb; and *tabulæ* the secondary object depending immediately on the *in* of the same. And I should continually impress upon him that the primary object was rendered by what *was called* the accusative; and the secondary object by what *was called* the dative. And I should consider such a simple and rational and intelligible way of parsing far better than the explaining the case of *tabulæ* by so ridiculous a rule, as

" *Verbs compounded with these ten prepositions,* AD, ANTE, CUM, IN, INTER, OB, POST, PRÆ, SUB, *and* SUPER, *govern a dative case.*"

And by and by, when my pupils were capable of following me, I should show them that in the termination of the accusative, in that insignificant letter *m* at the end of the word, was probably latent some preposition meaning *on*, *upon*, or *to*, which made the case to follow verbs or words of *motion* or *activity;* and that all datives properly ended in *i*, and that this *i* was probably the corruption of some preposition indicating *motion* or *rest*, *in* or *at a place;* and that all datives were really *locatives* or cases of *direction*.

And such explanations, instead of puzzling little heads, would amuse them and reassure them, by gradually bringing them to perceive that in Latin there was little of the mysterious, and that the people who once spoke that language were not all schoolmasters, but an ordinary mixture of people; tinkers and tailors, and wise men and foolish; like the inhabitants of our own island.

Meanwhile, if upholders of the system of rule-repetition argued against my plan as *unmethodic* and *vague*, I should reply that it were better for a boy to give *once*, in simple words that he understood, his explanation of a grammatical phenomenon, than to account for it *a thousand times* by a set formula that he understood partially or not at all. And I should assert that when a child has *once got a thorough mental grasp of a grammatical phenomenon*, he cannot let it go, though he try hard to do so; any more than an educated man, unless reduced to an unnatural imbecility, can forget that three times three makes nine, or that the three angles of a triangle are together equivalent to two right angles.

And I would add that it was with repetition, as with all things good and useful, quite possible to have too much of it. A child, if kept continually at a few airs upon the piano, will ultimately lose all sense of their melody; and a boy may repeat a grammar rule until it cease to carry an echo of meaning to his mind — and here I am boldly premising that it originally *did* carry a rather faint one. As in mental, so in physical operations, there are limits to the rule of repetition. We never heard of a boy forgetting to swim, or not learning to swim better, after he could once swim twenty strokes; or forgetting to skate, after having once skimmed over twenty yards on Duddingston Loch; *and that, too, although months and even years might have elapsed between two separate occasions of swimming or skating.*

VIII.

FROM PHÆDRUS TO FAREWELL.

IN my walk this afternoon I overtook some farm-servants, who were engaged in talk; and caught the following words, from a lassie, as I passed by: " *Well: I thocht* there WERE *a gate.*" And the sentence at once suggested itself as a simple example of the philological superiority of vulgar to literary speech. The Abstract Bagman would imagine there lay a blunder in the *were.* The real blunder is in his own *was.* The *were* is not plural, but an unconscious, traditional conservation of the old subjunctive, with its modification of vowel-sound. I should have, perhaps, only puzzled the farm-lassie, had I stopped to tell her that she was more than justified in putting her secondary verb into a mood of dubitativeness, seeing that the primary verb from its very signification precluded the idea of certitude in the dependent statement. Very probably, before my commendation had been closed, her sweetheart would have punched my head, under the idea that some indelicacy were lurking beneath my polysyllables.

But, *revenons à nos moutons*, whom we left browsing on Phædrus. As too early an acquaintance with metrical Latin is apt to confuse a child's healthy, natural ideas of the position of words, I should be at great pains to provide a corrective by spoken sentences, and the use of a good exercise-book, if I could procure one. Arnold's First Latin Composition-book is an admirable manual, but the price is so outrageously exorbitant, that I should hesitate in suggesting its purchase. However, if the book be dear, it is certainly good; and that palliation cannot be given for the majority of dear school-books. I could instance a very remarkable case of Selections from Herodotus. Taking the Tauchnitz standard of price as regards the mere ancient text, I should say there was about

two pennyworth of Greek in the bookling
I have in view: the notes might possibly
be worth a penny, and a paper-cover might
be got for the fraction of a farthing. The
book in question, to the disgrace of the
publisher or purchaser, costs four shillings
and sixpence. I would rather publish the
classics than teach them.

It is a very singular fact, that while we
confessedly use Latin as the chief instrument for inculcating clear and precise views
·on the philosophy of language, our pupils
are early made familiar with constructions
—especially in verse—where the simple
law of natural speech is violated in obedience to questionable rules of rhetoric, or the
imperious demands of non-Italian metre.
Take, for instance, the first line we meet
in opening our Virgil:

Tityre, tu, *patulæ* recubans sub tegmine *fagi.*

I would venture to affirm that the correct
way of translating this line is: *O Tityrus,
that reclinest beneath the shelter of the beech
when spreading;* indicating somewhat superfluously that the person addressed never
so reclined when the tree was bare, and

the weather, probably, damp or cold. Of
course it is obvious that *patulæ* is *intended*
as a mere epithet of *fagi*. But according
to all the rules of natural speech, ancient
or modern, the epithet should cling as
closely to its noun, as the bark to the tree,
the glove to the hand, the drapery to the
human form. And, whenever, such a dis-
location as the one above quoted takes
place, a novice should have explained to
him the reasons for the divorce of wedded
words; and should be informed that, what,
natural speech had joined together, foreign
metre had put asunder. Take another line:
a very beautiful one to an ear trained to
the abnormal licenses of Latin verse:

*Invalidas*que tibi tendens, heu! non tua, *palmas.*

Here our epithet and noun, that should be
as close together as the white legs of a toy-
soldier, are straddling like a Colossus, for
a fleet of petty words to sail under.

The second line of the elegiac stanza
sins continually against the rules of natural
arrangement; but the peculiar difficulty of
the metre pleads as a *circonstance atténu-
ante.*

But it is not in verse alone that a pupil
will stumble over artificial collocations.
They abound in prose, wherever a writer
is affecting the grand style, or is talking
fine; whenever Livy begins scene-painting;
or Cicero to roll in flood; or Tacitus to
"glower into a puddle;" or Juvenal to
pour the vials of his carefully-bottled wrath
upon excesses, with which he betrays a sus-
picious familiarity. A pupil, by being
brought into too early an acquaintance
with the tricks of rhetoric, fails later on to
appreciate their force. With a sober-tinted
background of natural Latin, these artificial
figures would be brought out in full relief;
as it is, they blend with the surrounding
landscape, and the whole picture, to the
art-student, has a dim and hazy look. If
a pupil throughout the whole course of his
elementary training were only or chiefly
conversant with easy-flowing constructions;
when he came, subsequently, upon the artificial arrangements of a rhetorical passage, their peculiarity would at once arrest
his attention; and the writer's end would
thus be attained; for it was just to arrest

a reader's attention that he arranged his words abnormally.

Furthermore, in sentences of spoken Latin, where the words should run in as natural an order as they do in un-rhetorical Italian, or, if you please, in common English, I should not hesitate to clip my adjectives of their terminations, wherever I could do so musically. Thus, I should not hesitate to say : *Bon' aurum 'st : non id, m 'ercule, bon' hominis 't ;* but in such a sentence as *Bona femin' erat mater tua,* I cannot clip the adjective before a consonant, as the Italian ear is abhorent of consonantal endings.

For a long while, then, I should, in all my spoken sentences, make my adjectives and nouns walk in loose pairs, side by side ; like the beasts into a Noah's ark, or school-girls in their joyless processions. In course of time, I should allow the adjective to throw its arms around its noun ; or make the couple touch finger-tips, as in a country dance, while their companion-words ran underneath.

When I had sufficiently guarded my

pupils against an unreasoning belief in unreasonable word-arrangements, I should
venture to put into their hands the exquisite Metamorphoses of Ovid. One or two
of the stories I should set aside, as victims
for sacrifice; or as scape-goats to be driven
into the wilderness of parsing. From these
our daily lessons for a time would be
chosen; and these lessons would be duly
construed, parsed, scanned, and committed
to memory. But I should from time to
time construe to them in uninterrupted
English some of the most interesting
stories; making comments as I went on, but
requiring no preparation, and no parsing.

Common sense would lead me to omit
several stories. Many, however, that Pru-
dery would pass by, I should exhibit in
all the exquisiteness of their naked grace.
I should follow Actæon through the wood,
until he came upon the fountain where
Diana was bathing, with her pretty hand-
maids round her. And I should ask my
boys, if *they* had ever surprised the goddess
and her nymphs in their watery revels;
and they would tell me that, in their holi-

days, on clear summer nights, in some lake among their own glorious mountains, they had seen the crescent-moon and the twinkling stars. And I would tell them, that the story had a moral meaning besides its poetic one; that, for all the poet said to the contrary, Actæon *was* led to the fountain by curiosity, and was punished for this fault, and not for a mere mistake. And they would agree with me that the moral was told in his story more gracefully, although not more funnily, than in their old favorite tale of Fatima and Bluebeard.

And I would follow with them the Holy Mother through the world, in her search of the lost Proserpine. And I would tell them, how in ancient Egypt Osiris died and came to life again, and was lost and was found; and that, though we had no Osiris in our northern climes, we had still our maiden Proserpine, that stood every spring-time in the fields with the poppies in her hair; and that she was stolen away every year still, and left for a while her mother desolate and forlorn.

And when they came to perceive what

truths of astronomy, morals, and religion
were quaintly and gracefully riddled in
sweet Latin rhythm, they would see that
the fancy of Ovid was not limited to indecent images, as it is supposed to have
been by the Tourist in Norway, and other
shallow writers of the Bagman tribe. And
if a member of this low caste ever came
into my class-room, I would call upon one
of the younger children to show him the
beauty and the truth of some story, wherein his impure imagination and defective
scholarship had seen only a never-intended
indecency.

But while in these readings I should
exact no preparation and no parsing, I
should exact a close and universal attention; and if the latter were not given by
any one pupil, I should consider the class
and myself as blameworthy, in failing, by
intellectual or moral means, to chain the
attention of the wandering pupil; and I
should punish the class and myself with the
loss of a quarter's play, for our selfish in-
attention to individual interests. And, by
and by, when I read a hundred lines to-

gether from a Latin poet; slowly and distinctly, and following closely the order of
Latin words with a due regard to honest
English idioms; there would probably not
be a boy in my class but would follow the
English rendering of every Latin word.
Acting upon this method, I have read
through the whole Æneid with a not very
advanced class in one year. For every
twenty lines they had construed, parsed,
and scanned, and said by heart, I read them
a hundred lines in current English; so that
they read two books in the year, and I read
ten. I believe they were the first child-
mariners in Great Britain that ever circum-
navigated that splendid poem.

Meanwhile, my pupils would have reached
the period when it is usual for boys to begin versifying. To see this process in all
its ridiculous nakedness, we should have
to visit one of the great English schools.
I have known young pupils to be removed
from Dunedin to Harrow, or Rugby, or
Marlborough, or other schools of fame.
Their parents have sometimes told me that
James or Willy was reported as doing very

well; only that he was very deficient in his
Latin verses. 1 remember a lady telling
me this, with a face of great concern, as
the report sent in of her own boy. This
boy of hers had a capital prose head, but
would turn a summersault as easily as a
pentameter.

Whilst I should impress upon all my
pupils, gradually but orally, the strict rules
of quantity and scansion, I should make
my verse exercises optional; and I should
not be surprised or annoyed if I found some
of my best boys unwilling to undertake
them, or, in their execution, coming below
their ordinary standard of intelligence.

And now, Reader, I would willingly draw
you on with me through an initiatory course
of Greek; and show you how interesting
and amusing may be made the study of its
regular declension and conjugation; how
the bare branches of its rudiments may be
clothed with green leaves; how with the
besom of common sense we should sweep
aorists and polysyllables underneath the
schoolroom grate. Or, leaving grammar on
the ground-floor, I would fain carry you

along with me up our Greek staircase to
Plato and Æschylus and Aristophanes in
the drawing-room, or to exercises in prose
and iambics in the garret. But, Reader,
how can I hope to retain you so long, when
I fail to retain my own pupils? If I begin
my march at *Penna* with half a hundred
little privates, before the march is ended
my company has been eight times deci-
mated, and a sorry decade is left for the
closing of the campaign. Some have fallen
by the way, and been buried in lawyers'
offices, or counting-houses, or beneath bank-
counters. Some have deserted, and gone to
serve commanders, who give them a finer
uniform and less toilsome work. .

I met the other day a former pupil, whose
school-fellows are still under me : he stopped
to shake me by the hand, and I was delighted to see him, for, though his talents
were below mediocrity, he was a well-con-
ditioned, manly little fellow. If he were
still in his old school-class, he would probably be a successful candidate for the last
place but one. I asked him what he was
now engaged in, and he told me, somewhat

nervously, that he was attending the class
of Logic and Metaphysics. And this reply
of his set me thinking, Reader, of that
wondrous chain of gold that binds to one
another all things in nature, animate and
inanimate; how the green grass grows upon
the idle hills to feed the silly sheep; how
the silly sheep browse thereupon to fatten
you and me; and how the great round
world, with its green hills, and its silly
sheep, and all its boys and schoolmasters,
is bound by the chain of gold fast to the
throne of Zeus. So, looking into that frank
and pleasant face, I thought: "Well, my
boy, thou art not living altogether in vain.
When thou quittest this thy bleating-
ground, thou wilt leave some tags of wool
behind thee. And the fleece of thy modest
fees will cover with an over-coat the learned
form of a most excellent professor."

IX.

TEETH ON EDGE AND CLOSED LIPS.

THE Cardinal of Westminster has the reputation of being the best Latinist of all that now wear violet stockings. What an interesting experiment it would be to kidnap his Eminence with the ambassador from Athens into the Cambridge senate-house, when the annual prize exercises were being read in Latin and Greek verse. I take it for granted that the Cardinal, from the sacredness of his calling, has somewhat of the Heraclitus in his composition; and that the ambassador, from the vivacity of his nation, will sympathize more with the laughter of Abdera. I can imagine that his Excellency would listen wonderingly during the recital of The Greek Ode; and, on hearing that it was in his own language, would burst, in spite of his good-breeding,

into an uncontrollable guffaw. Before the
Latin hexameters had gone through twelve
lines, the Cardinal would be removed to the
Lodge of Trinity, and treated soothingly
for a temporary derangement of the diges-
tive organs.

Were you ever present, Reader, at the
public distribution of prizes at a great English school? If so, you will have heard the
senior pupils recite what are called Alcaics
and Elegiacs, with a thin, scrannel-pipe pronunciation, and a mechanical observance of
the skeleton-rules of scanning. This is not
their fault. Some of these lads have musical ears; most of them can hum "God save
the Queen;" and all are quite aware that
they are uttering sounds as harmonious as
if one whistled on the edge of a comb. Not
their fault at all. They are taught *by us*
to read a most exquisitely musical language
in this barbarous way. You may hear the
Italian flute played in such a manner as to
resemble a split fife, by the public orators
at our great universities.

At a time when Greek was becoming the
language of the civilized world, and enter-

ing as the first linguistic element into the
education of youth, a grammarian of Alex-
andria suggested the idea of *accentuating*
all Greek words, as a help in the study of
a very intricate tongue, and as a means for
conserving its traditional rhythm. A few
such accents you may see in books of modern times; French, Italian, and Spanish.
To a native, or a foreigner thoroughly conversant with Greek, such multitudinous
accents as a page of Greek now exhibits are
blots upon the original text; and you may
imagine how they would have appeared to
an Athenian of the time of Pericles, by observing the effect upon yourself of the following style of printing:

> Thè cúrrent thàt wìth géntle múrmur glîdes,
> Thoû knôw'st, beîng stópp'd, 'ĭmpátiently dòth rûge.

These marks might be of some assistance
to a young Hindoo student of English, but
they would, in all probability, have pre-
vented Shakespeare from recognizing his
own handiwork. They give the appearance
of poetry severely scarred with the small-pox.

However, the ingenious invention of the
old grammarian has met with a fate that no

oracle, by any possibility, could have prognosticated. His accents, *even where they are questionably correct,* are carefully preserved in writing, and the rules upon which they proceed are sedulously studied, although their study is a somewhat perplexing one; but strange to say, they are never observed in the way he must have had in view, — we never sound a single word according to their suggestions, *except by chance.* We have a leader in our Greek concert, who flourishes his bâton vigorously, and in what is thought correctest time, but the members of the orchestra are independent of his rule, and regardless of one another.

Towards the close of my school-days, I used to envy very much my best of schoolfriends the privilege he enjoyed of supping from time to time with the greatest of then living writers. I remember his describing to me how this veteran scholar read an ode of Horace after the pronunciation he had recently heard in Tuscany; and I confess that until I had heard the simple but sweet music of the Italian vowels, I had had no idea that the Roman lyre could be struck to such reverberant sound. Indeed, I had always imagined that the cadence of Latin poetry resembled the intermittent notes of the piano, and I found, to my surprise and pleasure, that it admitted of the prolonged vibrations and rolls of the violin and organ. Perhaps in no piece of Latin poetry is the fulness of Italian sound, and the thinness of our own, more readily appreciable than in that Latinest of Latin poems, the Atys of Catullus. If any English scholar can succeed in making this poem sound musically in the ears of man, woman, or child, with our orthodox accentuation, he will have rivalled that ingenious German youth who produced the sounds of half an orchestra from a combination of Jew's-harps.

But, if our English pronunciation of Latin be unmusical for verse, it is absolutely ludicrous for prose, and the more so as the prose approaches the familiar and conversational style. We have but to read a scene of Plautus out loud, or to see one travestied at Westminster, to convince ourselves of this fact. For the purposes of carrying on an extempore conversation, our method of pronouncing is as ill-adapted as our system of teaching. But it will be argued that there would be no utility in a scholar's possessing the power of fluently speaking either of the old languages; that they are taught merely as abstract studies, for the purpose of conveying strict ideas of grammar and philology; that the mere sound of vowels and the accentuation of words are but trifles compared with the intellectual end in view.

I freely acknowledge that the heads of our greatest English schools are boldly self-consistent. They unflinchingly extend their system to modern languages; and I could name more than one flourishing and aristocratic school, where French is taught by an English clergyman with an accent that would set a Parisian coiffeur in convulsions; where every *u* is sounded like the *u* in *flute*, and every final *n* is clenched with an honest, Teuton guttural.

In his sixth year of tuition, a very excellent pupil left me for one of the most famous of southern schools. He was at the time

well advanced in French and German.   He
went south, I was told, to acquire an English
accent.   He went south, I know, to lose
that of French and German.   The latter
language he was advised to discontinue, as
it interfered with the more important study
of Latin versification.   The study of French,
however, *is* continued for him by an Englishman, with a sort of club-footed pronunciation.   "Oh, never mind his German,"
said the Vice-Principal, — who, strange to
say, is an excellent modern linguist, — to
my pupil's father; "he can pick it up *in six
weeks* (*!*) after he has left us."   I think it
must have taken about the same time for
the clergyman of that establishment to pick
up *his* French, with its club-footed and
hoof-like accentuation.

Now, Reader, reflect for one moment
upon the paradox that is presented to us.
We have two languages, Greek and Latin—
neither of which has ceased to be spoken in
continental Europe; two languages, which
have become our chief instruments of
higher education, *irrespectively altogether of
the chief end of any language;* to wit, the

expression of thought by speech. There is a good deal of tomfoolery in the teaching of many of our boarding-schools; but I have never yet heard of any enterprising and philosophical German illustrating to young ladies a course of musical lectures by means of a violin that went *thud-thud*, and a piano that went *jingle-jangle*.

I once dined with a friend, whose rooms were in the house of a *patissière*, who gave lessons in pastry-making to a class of young ladies. I formed a good idea of her didactic system from the indigestibility of a pie-crust, which was served up in my honor; for, detecting the hand of a novice in the pastry, I inferred that the teacher's method was strictly practical; and indeed, at the time, I selfishly regretted that it was so.

Again, good Reader, reflect for another moment upon another paradox. Let us suppose that by advertising, or some other omnipotent means, we could obtain a nursery-maid, a housemaid, and a cook, who could all speak Latin; and that your little daughter, from the age of seven to nine, should hear them daily conversing in her

nursery. Why, in two years she would talk
Latin as fluently as you talk English. Now,
do you suppose that the power of speaking
it with ease would be a barrier to her understanding the theory of its grammar? Or
will you venture to affirm that this imper-
ceptibly-acquired power would not be a very
powerful assistance to her and you, if you
should ever carry her in that language to
the analytic study of its syntax? Well,
Reader, you have, I will suppose, a son, who
has been acquiring an English accent, and
a partial control over the elegiac metre in
some public school; say for the last six
years. When he next dines at home, take
him unawares at dessert-time, and offer him
a guinea if he can express the following sentence in correct Latin: " I have been learning Latin for six years; and, upon my
word, I don't think I could, in that language, say *Bo* to a goose." Your guinea
will be quite safe. But if your little daugh-
ter has had a French governess for six
months, a similar experiment in French
would be attended with some risk.

A member of my own family, who received his early education in Florence, and graduated very recently at our Edinburgh University, was making a tour of Holland during the last summer. He had introductions to some of the chief medical professors in Utrecht. He went through the various wards in the hospital with the Professor of Clinical Surgery and his posse of students. *For an hour and a half*, the Professor, out of compliment to the stranger, made every remark to his students *in Latin*. And instead of giggling, or nudging each other, the students took notes, and seemed to follow with ease all that was said. And, what is more curious still, the stranger followed all the remarks made, as easily as if they had been given in English, French, Italian, or German, although his Latin studies had been discontinued at a much earlier period than when a scholar usually leaves an English school for the University. But then, in boyhood and early youth he had studied Latin with a view of reading it with ease and speaking it with fluency, and not with a view of writing stilted prose, trashy hexameters, and trashier alcaics. In fact, Latin had taken its part with other studies in rendering him an accomplished man, and had not been used in excess for the purpose of stuffing him into an useless University Prize Pig.

Now, Reader, not to speak of our schools of medicine, do you think you could find any Englishman, even after twenty years spent in teaching Latin, who could do with an effort what was done without an effort by this unscholastic Dutchman? Or, if you could hit upon such a native Phœnix, do you think he could gather a class, not of medical students, but of first-class Triposmen, who could follow him for half an hour?

And now, Reader, I fear I have tried your temper too far. Confess it. You are a *little* angry with me. "Do you mean to say, a true Briton is not as good as a Dutchman?" Nay, Reader, nay: I am as national as yourself. In *all* departments of science, and in *a few* branches of polite learning, our countrymen can hold their own against all Continentalists. But there is no doubt that, in *the familiar handling* of the classic tongues — of Latin especially — we are far behind Germany, Holland, and Italy. And the simple reason is that they, to a certain extent, follow nature in their method of teaching at least one of these languages; and make it, to some extent, a living language by their method of communicating it. With our present system of teaching, and our impossible pronunciation, any attempt at a practical use of the same language would present the ghastly phenomenon of galvanism upon a corpse.

Is there any chance then of amendment in our great public schools? In those of England, I think there is none; in those of Scotland, there is a possibility of change.

The fact is, the Reformation, that improved religion in England, spoiled its Latinity; and the pedantic dread of false quantities has strangled Italian accent. In Scotland, a servile imitation of what is bad in English scholarship has nearly led to the extinction of a music, which, at the commencement of the present century, might have been heard in every parish-school.

And now, your *Clerico-didaskalos* of England is a plump and comfortable blackbird.

who, from over-feeding, has forgotten his
ancient song. His lay-brother of the North,
however, is a thrush, who is kept on very
wholesomely-spare diet. Cover his cage
with a towel: let him wait a while for his
seed; and my goodness, how that hungry
bird will sing!

X.

PLACE AUX DAMES.

OUR sex is incorrigible. Eighteen centuries of Christianity have rained upon it with no permanently softening result. We speak of the feudal times as the dark ages; a title coined by the after-envy of a more logical, but more vulgar civilization. For some three hundred years there *was* a dim light in Christendom; and warriors, superfluously helmeted, with sword and battle-axe dinned into each other's heads a proper respect for the ladies. But in an unhappy hour, the Medicis of Florence made fashionable the study of Greek; and since Europe has taken to learning and logic, it has lost one-half of its old fun, and nearly all its old chivalry.

Strange to say, the most barbarous tribes we have ever unearthed, seem as deficient

in politeness as the most civilized and refined of western nations. But your bar-
barian is, at all events, no hypocrite. In
the old Mexican hut, the unheeded squaws
would in silence chew the narcotic weed
whose subsequent chewing was to make
their lord as like a pig as alcohol can make
a Christian. An African monarch fattens
his mistress out of all shape; not, as travellers say, to humor a low sense of female
beauty, but in obedience to the impulse of
a deeply-rooted male jealousy. The Turk
immures his wives in a dull Harem, and
feeds them on sickening sweetmeats, in revenge for the loss of a paradise, that he
would be too stupid to enjoy. The China-
man squeezes the feet of his women into
lumps of helplessness; but the more ingenious European transfers the pressure to
the female brain.

You will wonder, Reader, what spirit of
impertinence leads me to meddle with the
arcana of our Boarding-schools. I am quite
aware that I have no more right to pry into
the mysteries of a lady's education than into
those of her toilet. But I cannot help

hearing what I hear; seeing what I see. In every street I pass wonderingly beneath overshadowing domes of crinoline; and dainty silken stays peep out of the windows of that shop in George Street, which is, I believe, termed a *Magasin* from the inflammatory and inflammable nature of its contents. In another shop-window in that same street, I often see what are called OBJECT CARDS, which were invented by some spiteful, and, of course, male wretch, for the purpose of frittering away the time and intellects of all subsequent generations of girldom. To one of these cards I saw attached a small piece of coal, and underneath it was printed a farrago of chemical and other gibberish, which goes by the satirical name of " useful information." To another was attached a piece of sponge, too small to clean a slate, but apparently large enough to absorb a whole page of wishy-washy observations. To another was pinned a butterfly's wing. I am convinced that, inside the shop, I might have seen cards, illustrative of natural history, ornamented with impaled cockroaches and nasty martyred earwigs. What do instructors of young girls do with these cards? Do they read out loud the nonsense written underneath, as texts for informational sermons? And, in doing so, can they retain their gravity? If they have such command of facial muscle, O why do they waste in a school-room those talents for low comedy, which would win them renown and fortune at the Adelphi?

I heard, only a few days since, that our girls were fed upon *Latin roots.* I asked through what process of cookery these roots might have passed. I was informed that they were invariably given raw. Such indigestible food I knew to be fit only for pigs. And my blood boiled within me, to think that such should be the dewless nurture of the sweet acorn-cups of future womanhood; the pretty embryo-possibilities of maternity; that such copper-handling should be made of the silver pieces of small change, whose universality makes the golden guinea of a Madonna.

Then, again, I have heard of globes, whose use is taught in secret. I wonder

how they use them. Do they roll them up
and down their schoolrooms? or toss them
up, to catch them in gigantic cups? or, more
gracefully than acrobats in the Circus, pat-
ter them with pretty feet up and down inclined planes?

But, my little lady-reader, if you have
mysteries in your Boarding-school, so has
your brother at Rugby, and your cousin who
is preparing for examination at the Horse
Guards. The former is improving into
Alcaics the aphorisms of Tupper: the latter
is gathering universal history from the pic-
tured page of a Chepmell. O little Reader,
did you ever study the work of this great
historian? I wish I had a portrait of him.
I should hang it over my mantel-piece in an
inverted position; which position I should
alter to the natural one, so soon as I should
fall in with one individual who could make
head or tail of his cui-earthly-bono writings.

Music is supposed to be a *sine quâ non* in
the education of all girls. The boarding-
schools of Dunedin are allowed a very high
position in the field of feminine didactics;
for Dunedin is the intellectual capital of an

education-loving kingdom. In one of our
very fashionable and aristocratic schools
you will see a music-master, in the course
of three hours, pass fifteen little strumming
maidens through his hands. He gives this
lesson, of superintendence it is called, once
a week. In another still more fashionable
school this electric-telegraph superintendence is given once a fortnight. In twelve
minutes the master has to hear an old lesson
played, to settle the piece for the next lesson, to write a good or bad mark in a note-
book, and occasionally to take a pinch of
snuff, or blow his weary nose. The little
pupil, in the latter school, has about eleven
minutes of male-supervision in the course
of a fortnight; which would give fifty-five
seconds per diem, if the work were dis-
tributed over all the week-days. Have
these music-masters never heard of Rich-
ardson's Theatre, where a tragedy, a comedy, and a comic song are all enacted within
the limits of their perspiring lessons?

May not this electric-telegraph system
of musical instruction explain the general
shallowness of our drawing-room music?

The fault can hardly be in the brains or fingers of our girls, for they came of a race that has produced the most exquisite ballad-system and the best collection of love-songs in all Europe. Some thousands of our girls are studying music year by year; yet for every girl-musician in Dunedin you would find thirty in less populous Brussels, and ten in insignificant Bruges. And what are Belgian girls to the girls of Scotland?

Modern languages are taught at all schools to all pupils. How often, Reader, have you met with a girl of fifteen who could write French correctly, or speak it with a good accent; although she might have studied the language for four years at a flourishing school? This is not the fault of our girls: the cause lies deeper. Our boarding-schools are too often mere business speculations, whose proprietors have as much real interest in the mental culture of their charges as a hotel-keeper in the spiritual welfare of his guests: men of talent are often employed by them in work degrading to themselves and useless to their pupils; and very often sharp and ready fellows are employed, that never received the education of gentlemen, and were never intended to address a lady without the intervention of a counter. If a system is vulgar that employs incompetency, that sweats and underpays talent; is there no vulgarity in those patrons whose call for cheap teaching is the source of all the mischief? What do we want with your fine musicians and over-educated scholars? Give us teaching-stuff that will stand wear and tear; catgut nerves and gutta-percha brains!

Your German master is often a man of learning, and is always well educated: your French master of the old school was a man of elegant accomplishments and a *preux chevalier;* but the manners of France appear to have degenerated under the ell-wand of a Shop-king, and the spurred boot of a Barrack-emperor.

Italian—beautiful, musical, classic Italian — is, alas! not very generally appreciated, although its teachers are usually men of a high caste. Not long ago, a royal Prince at Holyrood read, for a while, Italian with an accomplished soldier and gentleman;

and this circumstance raised in the estima-
tion of our citizens the language of Dante,
Ariosto, Tasso, and Alfieri. What a good
thing it would be if we were honored with
a mere εἴδωλον of royalty in the old palace,
whose shadowy Highness might be represented as patronizing, from time to time,
such accomplishments as we seemed in
danger of forgetting! And it would not
be a change to be deplored, if we could
hear more music from the Italian nightin-
gale, and a trifle less of chatter from the
magpie of France.

But after all, modern languages should
be taught practically and conversationally.
The only grammar taught to girls below
the age of twelve should be that of their
own language; and its terms should be
made as plain and intelligible as possible.
Perhaps no subject is better taught than
this latter one in our schools. But to girls
of superior intelligence, even English is not
the language upon which to found general
and comprehensive ideas of grammar, such
as may facilitate the after-acquisition of
any modern language. You would never

inculcate ideas of filial duty on a child, by
continually obtruding upon him impertinent
mention of his own parents. You would
tell him amusing and instructive stories of
other children and *other* parents. Even so
with grammar.

In the education of boys, it has been
agreed, perhaps truly, that Latin is the best
instrument for inculcating the general laws
of language. Are there genders in educational systems, like as in Latin or French
nouns? Is there anything in Latin grammar peculiarly *male?* How did they talk
at dinner-time in ancient Rome? Did the
men speak only masculine nouns; the ladies,
feminine ones; and the servants, *common*
ones? We have no warrant for such a conclusion. I believe the Latin language to
have been, and still to be, incapable of such
partitioning. It is not of the masculine
gender; nor of the feminine; nor of the
neuter or neither; but, like other languages,
of *the either gender*. And, if properly taught,
it would be found a far easier language than
German; considerably easier than French;
and a little easier in its old form than in

its slightly altered form of modern Italian, which is very easy indeed.

Heaven forbid that our girls should be taught Latin with the grammars now in use, and those annotated books, that may help an incompetent master over an occasional stile, but can only enervate a pupil's brain, and transfer coin from the pocket of an exasperated parent to the pocket of an undeserving publisher.

I assert that a good Latin grammar might be limited to twenty-four pages, and sold, with a large profit, for sixpence; and that this bookling, with an extra outlay of half-a-crown, might, with a competent master, carry scholars over two years of work. And I also assert that girls might, with great advantage, pass through two or even three years of Latin teaching, if that language were taught on an easy, simple, and natural method.

Although a schoolmaster of boys, Reader, I have still a touch of gallantry. Smile at my proposal. I would undertake to teach Latin to a class of girls twelve years of age, without the use of pedantic and expensive books, or of pedantic and meaningless gram-

mar rules. My pronunciation would be
Italian, as nearly Tuscan as I could make
it. I would never forget that I was training children, not to be school-mistresses,
but gentle ladies in a drawing-room, and
gentler mothers in a nursery. I would so
teach a young class, that if a master of a
great English school were to interrupt us
in our work, he would say: "Ah! they are
engaged in a lesson of trumpery Italian."
And I would, perhaps, mildly quiz him to
my pupils in correct Latinity, which, from
being rapidly and musically spoken, he
would not understand. And in two years,
perhaps; and in three years, most certainly ·
I would have girls on my class, who would
speak an old language, not unlike the language of modern Tuscany, in a way that
would shame their brothers and cousins,
who had been five years at any grammar-
school in the kingdom, and trained on the
old system of Elementary Unintelligibility.
And I would teach them Latin in such a
way, that very soon they would read a parable in either Italian or Spanish without
stumbling over either word or construction.
And I would engage to say that my pupils

would like their work, and would not dislike their master.

And consider the collateral effects of so bracing and healthful an education of our girls. Boy-classics would be forced, in emulation, to dispense with much of their dull pedantry: and youths would be ashamed to continue ignorant of modern tongues that their sisters spoke with elegance and ease. We have now a smattering of youths that cram reluctantly some knowledge of French, German, Italian, or Spanish, to win marks in our Chinese examinations. What a vulgar and profane usage of the dialects of Corneille, Goethe, Dante, and Cervantes!

But, Reader, you are alarmed. You are afraid that such a system would make Blue-stockings of our girls. Prejudice, Reader: unmanly, unchivalrous prejudice. The ladies of the Russian noblesse can speak almost every language of Europe; but they are exquisitely feminine. My brother sat for a week opposite a fair creature at a *table-d'hôte* in Venice; and perhaps he never eat less, or enjoyed dinner more, for a week together. He heard her speak all the languages he knew; and some that he did not know. But for her linguistic powers, he would have taken her for an English girl, from her English accent and her blonde beauty. Of course, she was a Russian. She had no appearance of the Blue. If she was one; then I could wish that all were even as that sweet, young, blue-eyed polyglot. 'Twas a lucky fellow, I should think, that caught that little Tartar.

Do, Reader, disabuse your reasonable mind of unreasonable crotchets. Women have just as keen intelligence as men; less powers, maybe, of abstract reasoning; but far finer perceptive and linguistic faculties. They need not be trained to exhaustive scholarship; but refinement of mental culture suits them, perhaps, even more than it does our own sex.

I imagine that the Lady Jane, who read her Phædo when the horn was calling, had as pretty a mouse-face as you ever saw in a dream; and I am sure that gentle girl was a better scholar than any lad of seventeen is now in any school of England or Scotland.

And once upon a time, Reader — a long, long while ago — I knew a schoolmaster and that schoolmaster had a wife. And

she was young, and fair, and learned; like
that princess-pupil of old Ascham; fair
and learned as Sydney's sister, Pembroke's
mother. And her voice was ever soft, gentle, and low, Reader: an excellent thing in
woman. And her fingers were quick at
needlework, and nimble in all a housewife's
cunning. And she could draw sweet music
from the ivory board; and sweeter, stranger
music from the dull life of her schoolmaster-
husband. And she was slow of heart to understand mischief, but her feet ran swift to
do good. And she was simple with the simplicity of girlhood, and wise with the wisdom that cometh only of the Lord,—cometh
only to the children of the Kingdom. And
her sweet, young life was as a Morning
Hymn, sung by child-voices to rich organ-
music. Time shall throw his dart at Death,
ere Death has slain such another.

For she died, Reader: a long, long while
ago. And I stood once by her grave; her
green grave, not far from dear Dunedin.
Died, Reader: for all she was so fair and
young, and learned, and simple, and good.
And I am told it made a great difference to
that schoolmaster.

XI.

SOLAR SPECKS.

DURING the last Summer Vacations, I
devoted ten weeks to the sedulous and uninterrupted study of Homer. I had repeatedly read both Iliad and Odyssey, but usually in detached books, with an intermixture
of other work, or in places where I knew at
least one living soul. I now gave literally
my whole thoughts and attention to the
rhythm and story of these splendid poems,
fondly imagining I might solve to my own
satisfaction some of the many riddles they
held involved.

It was not so much from the then unsat-
isfactory condition of my health, as from a
general conviction, founded upon observa-
tion and tables of statistics, of the ridiculous
brevity of human life, that I refrained from
the use of German commentaries. I was

also impressed with the idea that Homer could only be explained by Homer; that the answer to the riddle was to be found latent in the question. And I felt thankful that I had never read any tediously-learned book, in my own or any other language, that could warp my views or muddle my conceptions.

I need hardly say, that I did not read these poems according to the ordinary principles of scansion. Such a continuous narcotic would have been dangerous to my physical health, and would have kept me dormant through two of the finest months we have had for years. I contrived, to my own satisfaction, to combine the rules of metre with those of accent; and in my pronunciation of the words where the vowel-sounds of modern Greek seemed thin, I adopted without hesitation the richer vowel-music of Italy.

I may as well premise that, as I read for my own selfish amusement, I did not hold myself bound to any code of laws, metrical or accentual. Thus when the old grammarians accentuated ἀνθρωπον on the first syllable, and ἀνθρωπους or ἀνθρωπους on the second, I disagreed with them, and ac centuated both words alike on the first syl lable, in defiance of all authority, ancient or modern. And I argued thus: If the mere addition of a plural *s* were to modify the accent of a word, then such a word as *milités* or *militems* might be expected to be other wise accentuated than *militem;* which would *seem* absurd: and whilst we say *mánnikin, whírligig, cóckle-shell*, we might expect to find *manníkins, whírligigs, vocklé-shells;* which would *be* very absurd indeed.

Of course, I should not be so peremptory in dealing with such words as ἀνέϱωπου, ἀνέϱωπῳ, for in the last syllable of these words are latent *two* distinct vowel sounds; and the words may have once been of the forms, ἀνέϱωποεϰς, ἀνέϱωποῖν; or some thing of the kind. Even in these words, however, I am inclined to be a little skepti cal. At all events, I should never speak of a deficiency of *ápples* in an *applé-pie;* or of cleaning my *chímney* with a little *chimnéy- sweep*.

From these and similar considerations, while I followed the received rules for accentuation to a very great extent, I ventured to contravene them on those not rare occasions, when they seemed to me intrinsically ridiculous. And in these cases, it appeared to me that the old grammarians having laid down laws of accentuation that were generally true, adhered rigidly to them on all occasions; forgetting the wise saying, that must have been old even in their day, that *there is no rule without an exception.*

During the course of my reading, I translated, *for the first time in my life,* some passages of English verse into Greek hexameters. I shall append them to the present article, by way of substantiating an assertion already made, that an enthusiastic student will fall naturally into an imitation of a favorite author, without the help or annoyance of years of specific training. Should they be considered as inferior in kind, the most inveterate opposer of school-reform will give me credit for frankness in submitting my arguments and their proofs, to his logic for refutation, and to his scholarship for suggestions of improvement.

Meanwhile, I was heaping up a pyramid

of laborious notes. I had classified the words that occur once or twice or thrice in the two poems; innumerable instances of irregularity in tense and mood; natural confusions of number and construction; the recurrences of special cadence in metre with a view of discovering the *tune* or *tunes* of the old Singers; the names of mountains and rivers, with a view of tracing Celtic synonyms; the similes, with the vain hope of bounding the scope of the poet's imaginative experience; the description of wounds, with the view of defining his knowledge of anatomy; peculiarities in the collocation of words, with the view of tracing the extent of his artificiality; irregularities of case-ending, which, commencing with the noun, would naturally extend to its imitators, the adjective and participle; and innumerable instances of verbal forms, which grammars and lexicons call passive, but whose reflective meaning may be thoroughly and idiomatically rendered by the Saxon auxiliary *get*. These notes cost me two months of hard work to write, and three subsequent months of moderate work to arrange in order.

But O the vanity of human toil! My fondest and my most humble hope is, that my boy may one day be a scholar, and a devout and enthusiastic student of the poet whose poetry to me is only equalled by the music of Mozart and Beethoven. And, behold, I was preparing a dull, ponderous book, which he might hereafter consider it a pious duty to peruse ; and which might possibly throw a dulness not their own into the works they were tediously illustrating. Furthermore, I called to mind how the reading of such annotations had transformed many a healthy scholar into a dreary pedant; and how the writing of the same had turned many a pedant into a Bishop. And I trembled for the safety of my own lay-estate; and saw the risk I was running of being ordained without a word of warning, and of being hurried away, unprepared, into the House of Lords, to preside, as a father in God, over a gigantic church-establishment, and, as a temporal peer, over the destinies of a great nation. I determined, therefore, to conceal my perilous intimacy with heathen particles and metres, καὶ λανθάνειν Ἑλληνισθείς. Accordingly, I surrendered my note-bundles to my good landlady; who, unwittingly, for a week past, has, in kindling her kitchen fire, been extinguishing my first and last chance of a book-stall immortality.

With regard to the main subject of the Iliad, I was convinced that it was the glory of Troy, and that Hector was the real hero of an Ionian poet's fancy. The commencement of the first book seemed to me worded with an exquisite artfulness, with the view of throwing the reader off his guard. As Ilium *did* fall, it was requisite for the poet to make it fall without honor to the victors. One of the latter is therefore selected as the type of beauty, strength, and passion; the undeserving favorite of unreasoning Fortune and partial gods. He is kept out of view for a very long while, to give his colleagues the opportunity of showing themselves inferior to the real hero. The absence is due to a prolonged sulkiness, occasioned by the loss of a feminine companion, to whom he does not appear to have been chivalrously attached. He might have caught the measles from Thersites, had the tale been told in prose. It would have served him right; and have answered effectually the purpose of the story. He is eventually roused to action by the death of his friend, who, at the close of a summer's day, after the slaughter of some scores of Trojans, falls, as is not unusual with warriors, on the field of battle. The mock-hero is as brutal in avenging his companion, as though Hector had murdered him at a banquet, and Hecuba had served him up at supper as a dainty dish before old Priam.

The magnificent description of the Hephæstian arms all tends to glorify the hero against whom they were forged, and to detract from the credit of the wearer. The deceit of Athênê in the final combat puts the extinguisher upon the glory of Achilles, and makes a splendid martyr of his antagonist. And the whole poem closes simply and majestically, like a funeral march of Beethoven: " So bare they knightly Hector to his grave;" the kindest husband that ever loved and honored wife; the most

courteous gentleman that ever spake softly
to fair and frail lady; the tenderest father
that ever dandled boy-baby; and the sternest knight that ever struck with sword
round Ilium.

While in the Iliad the master-hand had
wrought a variety of war-songs into one
long, homogeneous recitative, I saw that
in the Odyssey he had had to deal with
subject-matter more homely and less con-
gruous. Some quaint old Bunyans had in
earliest times quaffed the cup of Circe on
the island of Æœa. And mariners, Ionian
and Phœnician, by winter fires had spun
yarns for the great Weaver to incorporate
in his imperishable web. And he, who in
his old age drew from music a solace for
light denied, had in earlier manhood been
a bright-eyed sailor; had in Tyre seen the
works of cunning sons of Moloch; had
heard upon the Nile of the hundred-gated
Thebes, and the gloomy River, and the land
of Shadows. But not in Italy had he seen
the cannibal Læstrygons; nor in Sicily
great Polyphême. This latter worthy was
never suggested by Tauric Sun-god, with

metal disc upon his head. No: the poet
had heard all about him in his childhood
from his dear old grandmother. And,
Reader, we have all seen him in our nurseries, where he is still at his old work of
crunching men's bones. For Polyphême is
but a Cyclops; and a Cyclops is but a
Κύκλωξ; and a Kyklo-oks is nothing but
our old friend, Goggle-eyes.

The reason why the Odyssey had, in
course of time, triumphed over other poems
that sang the return of other heroes, was
firstly due to the fact that a type of character was wanted to illustrate other qualities
than pride, obstinacy, and physical courage;
a type around which might naturally cluster
all that was beautiful, serious, pleasant or
ridiculous in common life; a type of the
roving, adventurous, cunning island-rover,
to contrast vividly with the somewhat
monotonous mailed heroes of the *Lay of
Great Hector*, or the *Lays of the Achœan
Kings*. Again, Ithaca was at a more convenient distance from Troy than Salamis,
or Agros, or Pylos, or Lacedæmon. Had
the poet selected the Telamonian Ajax in

preference to Ulysses, a premature gale or his own pigheadedness, might have hurried the hero into port at the opening of the second book.

After diligent and mature consideration of the metre, I came to the conclusion that it belonged to the *genus vertebratum;* that the spine was Saturnian, and the vertebræ trochees; that in the old Italian hymn of the Salian priests we have the almost amorphous form that, on the sea-board of Ionia, had developed into the Homeric epic. The first rude hymns and ballads would probably run to the following simple metre:

$$-\cup \mid -\cup \mid -\cup \parallel -\cup \mid -\cup \mid -\cup$$
$$-\cup\cup \mid -\cup\cup \mid -- \parallel -\cup\cup \mid -\cup\cup \mid$$
$$\cup-\cup \mid \cup-\cup \mid \parallel \cup-\cup \mid \cup-\cup \mid$$

and it is a singular coincidence that the old Salii should have perambulated the streets of Rome, with the sacred shields, dancing to their hymn of

Æno' Las | os ju | vato.‖ Triumpe ! | Triumpe ! | Triumpe !

to a metre, and perhaps a music, not dissimilar to that of the Methodist's sweet

simple lines, the simplicity of which verges
on the ridiculous:

O but | that will be | joyful ‖ joyful | joy-y-ful | joyful,
O but | that will be | joyful ‖ when we | meet to | part no
  more.

Indeed, it occurred to me that all poetry
must resolve itself eventually into a system
of trochees or iambi; which feet are easily
interchangeable by a change of syllabic
emphasis. However, I felt convinced that,
in the Arian languages, the trochee emphasis would prevail, while a dialect preserved its rich vowel inflexions; that the
iambic emphasis would creep in, as a dialect began to use contracted endings; and
would, finally, be predominant, when the
dialect should take to the use of prefixes
and the disuse of vowel endings. Consequently, I was not surprised to find the
iambus in the Attic drama and Teutonic
modern epic; and the trochee dominant in
Dante, whose dialect has lost, indeed, its
case-affixes, but conserved its sweet vowel
terminations.

Now, in the skeleton metre above given,
a continuous sequence of trochees over a

long poem would be next to impossible; and, if possible, would be very unmusical. The dactyl would seem to me the natural efflorescence of the trochee; as the anapæst of the iambus. All metres of a ballad kind might be expected to show something answering to a refrain, or something analogous to our rhyme. I shall consequently expect to find in the above a dactyl towards the close of the line; not at the very end, as the effect would be jerky, and unsuggestive of repose; and not too far from the end, or else the echo would be lost. And this consideration explains to me the almost invariable presence of the dactyl in the fifth foot.

As for the spondees that occur, I hold that the majority of them were accentuated or read as trochees. They certainly would conduce to give variety to the metre, and at times to introduce a purposed stateliness and majesty. Very often they would intrude as the children of necessity.

From the extreme perfection of the metre in the two poems, and the *extreme inaccuracy in the use of conditional and dubitative moods,* it is obvious that the poems were brought to a completion in an age of high civilization.

Furthermore, we may guage the civilization of a poet by the use of the adverb, as we test that of a lady by the handling of a fork. For, as a musician once remarked to me, the adverb is the index of mental refinement. It is a Nilometer of rising taste. Your Helot has but a limited store of adverbs, but they are cayenne-ish, superlative. In a very simple and early ballad the adverb would scarcely appear at all. In Homer, it varies through *chiaro* to *chiar'-oscuro*, and again to *chiaro:* no *oscuro* or *oscurissimo;* for only an indifferent painter would heighten a contrast by the vulgar use of black. If the poetry of Homer is simple and primitive, then, maybe, painting at one stride achieved the Madonnas of Raffaelle and the sunsets of Claude.

To me the Iliad appears a congeries of warlike lays, grouped by the artifice of a most simple plot into a homogeneous story. The lays were in a rude Saturnian metre, and adapted for singing. The story is told in a stately but ever-varying measure, that flows in a majestic recitative. The Odyssey seems to have stolen from all possible sources; allegory, travellers' tales, and nursery-lore. The story is not homogeneous, but kaleidoscopic; as the story should have been that was destined to give birth to Jack the Giant Killer and Sinbad the Sailor; to lend grace to the Æneid, and majesty to Paradise Lost.

In both the poems, with more especial care in the Iliad, the primitive trochee system is modulated into the richer music of intermixed spondees and dactyls. For a long while the trochee would be found scattered through the metre, where of yore he was predominant; but at length he would fade away like a Red Indian before his stalwart supplanters. I am convinced, however, that a great many of the superfluous monosyllabic appendages, as τε and γε, are due to scribes, who carried on a war of extermination against the remnant of the old Trochees. I wish the Trochees had risen with a war-whoop and scalped them by the dozen.

Again; I am led to consider the Homeric

poems as the production of a high civilization, from the fact that they admit of an
abnormal position of words, as evinced,
chiefly, in the unnatural separation of epithet and noun. As this license, however,
is but *sparingly* used, I infer that the metre
of the poem was the gradual growth of
an autochthonous system of versification.
Thus, in a highly finished poem like the
sixth book of the Iliad, I only find in five
hundred and twenty lines about thirty instances where the position of words is questionable; and no instance where the position is very distorted.

But when I come to the examination of
the chief Roman poems, I find thirty instances of false position in the first eighty-
eight lines of Lucretius; in the first fifty-
one lines of the first book of the Æneid; in
the first sixty-four lines of the second book
of Ovid's Metamorphoses; and in the first
seventy-four lines of the second epistle of
the second book of Horace; in none of
which cases is the adjective in the predicate.
That is to say, while in Homer I find a
liberty taken with natural construction once

in every *eighteen lines ;* I find one taken in
every alternate line by the poets of and
about the Augustan age. And furthermore,
in these latter poets I find certain constructions, which for harshness have no analogue
in their simpler and grander metrical proto-
type ; as, for instance, in such lines as —

Quàm quœ Dardanium tellus mihi servat Acesten
Et *patris Anchisæ gremio* complectitur ossa.

Intereà, *medium* Æneas jam classe tenebat
Certus *iter.*

*Cæruleæ cui terga notæ maculosus et auro
Squamam incendebat fulgor.*

Cujus ebur nitidum *fastigia* summa tegebat:
Argenti *bifores* radiabant *lumine valvæ.*

Proteäque ambiguum, *balænarumque* prementem
Ægœona *suis immania terga lacertis.*

Inde loco medius *rerum novitate paventem*
Sol *oculis juvenem, quibus* aspicit omnia, vidit.

Jussa *Deæ celeres* peragunt, *ignemque vomentes,*
Ambrosiae succo saturos, præsepibus altis
Quadrupedes ducunt.

Occupat ille *levem juvenili corpore currum.*

Utque labant *curvæ justo sine pondere* naves.

Tum primùm *radiis gelidi* caluere Triones.

                    Ita fertur, ut acri
Præcipiti pinus *Boreâ, cui* victa remisit
Frena suus rector.

Ille *relicto* —
Nam Ligurum populos et magnas rexerat urbes —
Imperio.

Luculli miles *collecta* viatica *multis*
Ærumnis, lassus dum noctu stertit, ad assem
Perdiderat.

Dura sed emovere loco me tempora grato,
Civilisque rudem belli tulit æstus ad arma.

Obturem *patulas impune legentibus* aures.

Obscurata diù populo bonus *eruet,* atque
Proferet in lucem speciosa vocabula rerum.

In each of the passages here quoted there
is a construction that spoken Latin would
have undoubtedly eschewed; and in some
of the passages, a strict and regular trans-
lation, independent of the context, would
make downright nonsense; and indeed, in
such Ovidian lines as

Non mihi, quæ duri colerent *pater* arva juvenci,
Lanigerosve greges, non ulla armenta reliquit,

we have an instance of a word being un-
grammatically choked by an accumulation
on all sides of relative mud. And remember,
these more than questionable passages are
culled from only about six pages, taken at
random, of the most finished Augustan verse.

The fact is, the sudden influx of Grecian

refinement had as brilliant and disastrous an effect upon Roman genius, as had the influx of Transatlantic gold upon the morals and political power of Spain. In the last generation of the Republic, and in the first of the Empire, men were in a hurry to acquire intellectual wealth, and paid the penalty for their imprudent haste.

Again; in Homer, the cadence of such a line as the following —

Τυδέος ἔκγονός ἐσσι, δαΐφρονος Οἰνείδαο,

recurs *once in every nine lines* on an average. Such a line occasionally occurs in Lucretius; but may be said to be non-existent in the Augustan poets. That is to say, Lucretius imitated the musical cadence of Homer, and the after poets followed the stricter rules of conventional scansion, which in all probability were wholly unknown to Homer. The rhythm of Lucretius is monotonous, but it is trochaic, dactylic, Italian. Catullus is more trochaic, more Italian. Virgil, Horace, and Ovid are more varied, more refined, and decidedly un-Italian.

That is to say, these three poets performed a feat completely unparalleled in the history of all plastic art. They had a somewhat unformed language to work upon, and used for their models the most finished works of the most perfect of all languages. Nay, they even insisted on burdening themselves with accuracies of rhythm to which their prototypes were strangers. And they so exquisitely moulded their rude language to the wished-for shape, that the licenses, taken with it in the process, have escaped the ken of all succeeding scholars and critics. Their very blunders have become the touchstones of elegance.

Lucretius, from the nature of his subject, addresses himself only to an esoteric set of readers; as do Virgil, Horace, and Ovid from the exquisite though unnational polish of their style. A Roman noble of good natural abilities, who had spent a few years at the University of Athens, would have enjoyed equally the grandeur of Lucretius, the sweet dignity of Virgil, the lyrical chastity and bantering wisdom of Horace, the wit and fancy and flexile adaptativeness of Ovid. But Catullus alone, with the trochaic and dactylic ring of his Italian hende-

casyllables and the unapproached native
force of his Atys, could have sent a thrill
to the heart of a shop-boy in Rome, or a
shepherd on the Calabrian hills.

The Augustan poets anticipated the due
season of metrical perfection; *præripuere
musicen postero sæculo debitam;* but they
warped their language in the process. Greek
mental wealth, a Mæcenas and an Emperor
ripened prematurely the delicious fruit;
and killed the seed. For Virgil, Ovid, and
Horace had no successors. There are passages in Juvenal that would lead us to
suppose he might have been a poet had he
never studied rhetoric. A green glade opens
at long intervals in the dreary wood of
Lucan. The dull lamps of Silius and
Statius flare up momentarily from time
to time. Claudian was a revolving light,
that sent a few intermittent gleams through
thick darkness, and went out after doing
little service. But a priest is to sit on the
throne of the Cæsars, and waves of war
are to surge over Italy. The old gods will
linger in remote places, and in the hearts
of common men: they are lingering there

still. The ancient speech will live in the
mouth of peasant-folk, safe from the pedan-
ticisms of an aristocratic literature, and
bending, undestroyed, before the hurri-
canes of war. After dark and stormy centuries, a Dante will sing to a Christian lyre
a song, grand and eternal as the Apen-
nines; in words of native, pure, indigenous
Italian; in a dialect older than the great
grandmother of the elder Cato.

Now, supposing we commenced our system of instruction in Latin upon a *vivâ-voce*,
conversational method, and approached Latin literature through natural passages of
prose, such as we might extract from Plautus
—ay, and from Erasmus—a pupil would detect instinctively the offences committed
against universal grammar by the polished
poets of the Augustan age. As it is, we ig-
nore altogether the conversational method in
our teaching, and profess to teach Latin only
for the inculcation of the rules of abstract
grammar; and the majority of the examples
to our rules of syntax are elaborate passages
from the most artificial class of all poets.

In other wards, we inculcate the rules of

abstract grammar by the aid of examples
where the rules of natural grammar are
ignored in favor of a style conventional
and artificial; and, to convey to young
children intelligible ideas of general grammar, we pass by with contempt the teaching
of their mother-tongue, and the lessons of
an easy-flowing, unconventional Latinity,
and puzzle their little brains by introducing
them at once to constructions, whose essential faultiness and conventional grace are
visible only to a trained and finished scholar.
Indeed, am I presumptuous in asserting,
that hitherto *all* our best Latinists have
gone repeatedly over Augustan ground,
never dreaming that it was riddled with
grammatical pit-falls? Nay; am I presumptuous in stating also that even Italian Latinists have passed unnoticed the flaws that, to
a certain extent, denationalize the master-
poems of their own ancient literature? If
I am presumptuous, Reader, I am so in a
good cause. I am not exalting my own puny
ideas of language against the taste and wit
and genius of the Augustan trio. The Hel-
lenized Latinity of these giants is splendid

enough — heaven knows!—in spite of, and perhaps by reason of, its foreign cadence and its daring disregard of simplicity. But, leaving to Horace the undisputed throne of Wit and Wisdom, I recognize in Ariosto the equal of Ovid, and in Dante one greater than the great Mantuan. And the fancy of Ariosto and the sublimity of Dante are of Italian growth, autochthonal. So, Reader, if I am presumptuous, I humbly hope this presumption will prove to be a malady incurable and contagious.

> Upon what meat hath our schoolmaster fed,
> That he is grown so big? Can Isis send
> No sallow, hungry-visaged Cassius north,
> To prick the veins of his o'er-swoln conceit!
> Come, envious Casca; thin-lipp'd Cassius, come;
> Draw near him, as he unsuspecting stands
> Before his pygmy, sycophant senators;
> And, hissing thro' your teeth, 'Take this, and that!'
> Stab him, as ye stabb'd Cæsar, with steel-pens!

XII.

MORTE D'ARTHUR.

So all day long the noise of battle roll'd
Among the mountains by the winter sea,
Until King Arthur's table, man by man,
Had fall'n in Lyonness about their Lord,
King Arthur: then, because his wound was deep,
The bold Sir Bedivere uplifted him,
Sir Bedivere, the last of all his knights,
And bore him to a chapel nigh the field,
A broken chancel with a broken cross,
That stood on a dark strait of barren land.
On one side lay the Ocean, and on one
Lay a great water, and the moon was full.

Πᾶν δ' ἦμαρ μάρναντο παρὰ ῥηγμῖνα θαλάσσης
χειμερινῆς, αἰεὶ δ' ἐν ὄρεσσι κυλίνδετ' ἀϋτή·
ὄφρ' ἕταροι βασιλῆος ἐν αἰνῇ δηϊότητι
πάντες ἐπασσύτεροι σφετέρῳ πέσον ἀμφὶ ἄνακτι,
'Αρτούρῳ· τότε δὴ βασιλῆα γὰρ ἕλκος ἔτειρεν,
ἀμφὶ δ' ἄρ' ὤμοιιν κρατερὸς Βεδύηρος ἀείρας
ἐξίφερεν πολέμου· ἑτάρων γὰρ ἔην ἰρτήρων
λοίσθιος· ὃς δὲ ἄνακτ' οὐ τηλόσεν ἦγε κατ' ἀκτῆς.
ἱρὸς ὅθι νηὸς σὺν κίοσιν ἦρτο ῥαγείσαις,
στῆ δὲ μελαμπέτρου δνοφερῷ ἐν στεινεῖ γαίης·
τῇ μέν τ' 'Ωκεανὸς μέγας ἔπλετο, τῇ δέ τε λίμνη
ἄσπετος. ἠδ' ἄρ' ὕπερθεν ἔην πλήθουσα Σελήνη.

ULYSSES.

The long day wanes: the slow moon climbs:
    the deep
Moans round with many voices. Come, my friends,
'Tis not too late to seek a newer world.
Push off, and, sitting well in order, smite
The sounding furrows; for my purpose holds
To sail beyond the sunset, and the baths
Of all the western stars, until I die.
It may be that the gulfs will wash us down:
It may be we shall touch the Happy Isles,
And see the great Achilles, whom we knew.
Tho' much is taken, much abides; and tho'
We are not now that strength which in old days
Moved earth and heaven; that which we are,
    we are;
One equal temper of heroic hearts,
Made weak by time and fate, but strong in will
To strive, to seek, to find, and not to yield.

ʿΗμαρ δ᾽ ἄνεται, ἀμβαίνει δέ τε δῖα Σελήνη
οὐρανὸν, ἠδὲ θάλασσα περιβρέμει ἠχήεσσα·
Εἰ δ᾽ ἄγετε, εἰς ἅλα δῖαν ἐρύσσατε νῆα μέλαιναν,
ὀψέ περ ἡλικίας ὄντες τ᾽ ἐπὶ γήραος οὐδῷ,
κληῖδεσσι δ᾽ ἐφεζόμενοι στονόεντα κέλευθα
τύπτετε· νῦν δ᾽ ἐμὲ θυμὸς ἐνὶ στήθεσσιν ἀνῆκε,
πόντον ἐπιπλείειν ὑπὲρ Ἠέλιον καταδύντι
καὶ Ζεφύροιο δόμους ἄστρων δέ τε καλὰ λόετρα,
ὄφρα με Μοῖρα κίχῃ θανάτου, βιοτόν τε τελέσσῃ.
Τίς δ᾽ οἶδ᾽, ἠέ κεν ἄμμε καταβρόξειε θάλασσα,
ἠέ κεν Ἠλύσιον πεδίον μακάρων δέ τε νήσους
ἱξόμεθ᾽, ἔνθα δ᾽ ἄρ᾽ αὖθις ἰδώμεθα Πηλέος υἱόν,
ὅς ῥα ποτ᾽ ἄμμιν ἔην περὶ Ἴλιον ἐσθλὸς ἑταῖρος.
Ἀλλὰ τάδ᾽ ἀθανάτων γε θεῶν ἐν γούνασι κεῖται·
πολλὰ μὲν οὖν ἀπόλωλε, μένει δέ τε πολλά· καὶ ἤδη,
εἰ καὶ γούνασιν οὐκέτ᾽ ἔνεστι μένος τε βίη τε,
ὡς ποτ᾽ ἔην, ἐπεὶ ἄμμιν ὑπέστενεν εὐρεῖα χθών,
ἐσμὲν δ᾽ οἷοί γ᾽ ἐσμέν· ἔνεστι δὲ θυμὸς ἀγήνωρ,
εἷς πάντεσσιν ὁμῶς, θέλομεν δ᾽ ἔτι πολλὰ παθόντες
τετλάμεν ἠδὲ φέρειν, ἀλλ᾽ οὔ τι μίνυνθά περ εἴκειν.

EDWIN OF DIERA.

WHILE the tale
Was being told, the people silent stood,
But at its close their grief broke out afresh,
When some fond memory brought back Regner's
     face,
His gait, his voice, some cordial smile of his,
And all the frank and cunning ways he had
To steal a gazer's heart.   The long day waned,
And, at the mournful setting of the sun,
Up through the valley came the saddened files,
With Regner's body borne on levelled spears.
And, when they laid the piteous burden down
Within the gate, with a most bitter cry
The loose-haired Bertha on it flung herself,
And strove, in sorrow's passionate unbelief,
To kiss dead lips to life.   The sternest lids
Were wet with pity then.   But when the King
Was, like a child, led up to see his son,
With sense of woe in woe's own greatness
     drowned, ·
With some obscure instinct of reverence
For sorrow sacreder than any crown,
The weeping people stood round, hushed as death.

Ὡς ἄρ' ὅγ' ἐν μέσσοισιν ἐτήτυμος ἄγγελος εἶπεν·
οἱ δ' εἵως μὲν σιγῇ ἀκουάζοντο λέγοντος·
ἀλλ' ἐπεὶ ἐς τέλος ἀγγελίης πεπύθοντ' ἀλεγεινῆς,
πᾶσιν ἐνὶ στήθεσσι πάλιν γόου ἵμερος ὦρτο,
μνησαμένοισι φίλου 'Ρηξήνορος ἱπποδάμοιο,
οἷός τ' ἦν φωνήν τε βάσιν θ', ὡς δ' ἡδὺ γέλασκεν,
ὥς τ' ἄρ' ἀλιτρὸς ἔην, καὶ ὅσ' οὐκ ἀποφώλια εἰδώς,
ὥς δ' ἑτάροις τ' ἀγανὸς λαοῖσί τε πᾶσιν ἐνηής.

"Ανετο δ' ἱερὸν ἦμαρ ἐπ' ἀνδράσι μυρομένοισι·
ἦμος δ' 'Ηέλιος κατέδυ, καὶ ἐπὶ κνέφας ἦλθεν,
οὔρεος ἀμβαίνοντες ἀνὰ πτύχας ἀσπιδιῶται
φαίνοντο στρωτῇσι δ' ἐπ' ἐγχείῃσι ταθέντα
ἀμφ' ὤμοισι φέρον 'Ρηξήνορα τεθνηῶτα.
Αὐτὰρ ἐπεὶ νεκρὸν κατέθεντ' ἔντοσθε πυλάων,
ὡς ἴδεν, ὡς ὀλόλυξεν ἐϋπλόκαμος 'Αρήτη,
ἀμφὶ δὲ χεῖρε βαλοῦσα κάρη τ' ἔκυσ' ἠδὲ πρόσωπα,
πείθεσθαι δ' ἐνὶ θυμῷ, ὃ δή ῥά οἱ αὐτὸς ὀλώλει,
νηπίη, οὐκ ἐθέλεσκεν· ἀνέστησεν δέ μιν οὐδ' ὥς.

'Η ῥα μὲν οὖν πάντεσσιν ὑφ' ἵμερον ὦρσε γόοιο·
αὐτὰρ ἐπεὶ πατέρ' αὐτὸν, 'Ερευθαλίονι αἰδοῖον,
ὀτρηροὶ θεράποντες ἄγον φίλον υἱὸν ἰδέσθαι,
δὴ τότ' ἄρ' ἀσχαλόων σφι γέρων ἐσεμάσσατο θυμόν,
καὶ σεμνὸς πολὺ μᾶλλον ἔεισατ', ἀκηχέμενός περ·
αἰδόμενοι δέ μιν ἔσταν, ἀκήν τ' ἐγένοντο σιωπῇ.

ENALLOS AND CYMODAMEIA.

SHE saw him in the action of his prayer,
Troubled, and ran to soothe him. From the
    ground
Ere she had claspt his neck, her feet were borne.
He caught her robe; and its white radiance rose
Rapidly, all day long, through the green sea.
Enallos loost not from that robe his grasp,
But spann'd one ancle too.   The swift ascent
Had stunn'd them into slumber, sweet, serene,
Invigorating her, nor letting loose
The lover's arm below; albeit at last
It closed those eyes intensely fixt thereon,
And stil as fixt in dreaming.   Both were cast
Upon an iland till'd by peaceful men
And few (no port nor road accessible)
Fruitful and green as the abode they left,
And warm with summer, warm with love and song
'Tis said that some whom most Apollo loves
Have seen that iland, guided by his light;
And others have gone near it, but a fog
Rose up between them and the lofty rocks;
Yet they relate they saw it quite as well,
And shepherd-boys and pious hinds believe.

Ὃς δὲ μέγ' ὀχθήσας τάδ' ἄρ' εὔχετο, χεῖρας ὀρεγνύς·
ἡ δέ μιν εὐχόμενον κούρη ἴδε, βῆ δὲ θεέσκειν,
μειλιχίοις ἐπέεσσι προσειπέμεναι μεμανῖα·
ἀλλὰ πρὶν ἠιθέῳ δειρῇ περὶ χεῖρας ἰάλλειν,
ποσσὶν ἀν' ἐκ δαπέδου ἰοειδέος ὦρνυτ' ἐλαφροῖς·
Ἦ ῥα πανημερίη σὺν Ἐνάλλῳ Κυμοδάμεια
ὦρνυτο κυανέοιο δι' Ὠκεανοῖο ῥεέθρων,
καρπαλίμως· ἑανοῦ δ' ἄρ' Ἔναλλος χειρὶ φαεινοῦ
εἴχετο δεξιτέρῃ, ἑτέρῃ δέ τὲ μιν σφύρου εἷλεν.
Ἀμφοτέροιν δ' ἅμα ὕπνος ἐπὶ βλεφάροισιν ἔπιπτε,
ῥήγρετος, ἥδιστος, θανάτῳ ἄγχιστα ἐοικώς.
Ἡ δ' οὖν, καὶ βρίζουσά περ, ᾖεν, ὁ δ' εἶχέ μιν αἰεί·
ὕπνου δ' οὐ χεῖρες μὲν ὑπὸ γλυκεροῖο λέλυντο,
αὐτὰρ οἱ ὀφθαλμοί γ' ἐπεπήγεσαν, ὡς ἐν ὀνείρῳ.
Ἤδη δ' ἀμφοτέρους μέγα πόντου κῦμα πέλασσε
νῆσον ἐπ' ἠγαθέην· ἐσθλοὶ δ' ἀρόωντό μιν ἄνδρες
παῦροί τ', οὐδ' ἐνέην τις ἀταρπιτὸς οὔτε λιμήν τις·
χλωρήν, ἠΰτε καὶ σφέτερόν γ' ὑπὸ βένθεσιν ἄντρον,
καρποφόρον· θάλψεν δέ τ' ἔμως, μολπή τε ἔαρ τε.
Φασὶν. δ' ὡς ποτὲ καὶ τινες, οὓς Ἑκάεργος Ἀπόλλων
τῖε μάλιστ' ἀνδρῶν, τήν γ' ὀφθαλμοῖσι ἰδέσθαι.
πρὸς δ' ἄλλοι ποτὲ καὶ πελάσαντ', ἀνέδυ δ' ἄρ ὀμίχλη
αὐτῶν μεσσηγὺς πετράων τ' ὀκριοέσσιν·
ἀλλὰ καὶ ὡς φάσκουσι ἰδεῖν τάδε· τῶν δέ τε παῖδες
ποιμένες εὐπίστως ἀροτῆρες τ' ἄνδρες ἄκουσαν.

THE DEATH OF ARTEMIDORA.

'Artemidora! Gods invisible,
While thou art lying faint along the couch,
Have tied the sandal to thy slender feet
And stand beside thee, ready to convey
Thy weary steps where other rivers flow.
Refreshing shades will waft thy weariness
Away, and voices like thy own come near
And nearer, and solicit an embrace."
  Artemidora sigh'd, and would have prest
The hand now pressing hers, but was too weak.
Iris stood over her dark hair unseen
While thus Elpenor spake.   He lookt into
Eyes that had given light and life erewhile
To those above them, and now dim with tears
And wakefulness.   Again he spake of joy
Eternal.   At that word, that sad word, *joy*,
Faithful and fond her bosom heaved once more:
Her head fell back: and now a loud deep sob
Swell'd thro' the darken'd chamber; 't was not
        hers.

Ερμείας δ' ἀκάκητα μάλα σχεδὸν ἤλυθεν ἤδη,
νωιτέροις δ' ἄρ' ἔην οὐκ ὀφθαλμοῖσιν ἐναργής,
εἵως τοῖσιδ' ἄκικυς ἐπὶ λεχέεσσι τάθησθα·
ἤλυθε, σοῖσι δ' ὑπὸ λεπτοῖς ποσὶ δῆσε πέδιλα,
πὰρ δέ σοι ἔστη νῦν, μάλα τειρομένην σε κατάξων
γαῖαν ἐτ' ἀλλοδαπὴν καὶ ἐπ' ἀενάοντα ῥέεθρα·
σοὶ δ' ἀνέμων λιαραὶ πνοιαὶ σκιόεσσα δὲ θ' ὕλη
ῥέα μάλ' ἀποψύξουσι πόνον τε καὶ ἄλγεα πάντα·
ψυχαὶ δ' ἀμφὶ περὶξ, γλυκύφωνοι ἴσά σοι αὐτῇ,
ἀγρόμεναι χεῖράς σοι ἀραιὰς ἀμφιβαλοῦσιν,

   'Η δ' ὀλιγοδρανέουσ' ὡς ἤθελεν ἀντιλαβέσθαι
δεξιτέρης· ἀλλ' οὐκ ἐδυνήσατο, ἱεμένη περ.
Τόφρα δ' ὑπὲρ πλοκάμοις ἰοειδέσι Ἶρις ἐπέστη·
ὃς δ' ἔτι ἐπ' ὀφθαλμοῖσιν ἰδέρκετο ἧς ἀλόχοιο,
κάλλεϊ δ' οἱ στίλβειν μιν ἐώθεσαν ἀγλαΐη τε,
ἐγρομένη δ' ἄρ' ὑπὸ στυγεροῦ καμάτοιο δαμάσθεν.
Δεύτερον αὖ πύματόν τε μιν 'Ελπήνωρ προσέειπεν·
'Η ῥά νυ θάλπωρή ἔσεται ψυχαῖσι καμόντων,
τέρψονται δέ που αἰεὶ ἐν ἀσφοδελῷ λειμῶνι.

   Ὡς φάτο· τοῦ δ' ἄλοχος φίλη ἔκλυεν αὐδήσαντος,
καὶ πύματον κραδίη οἱ ἐνὶ στήθεσσι πάταξεν·
εἴσατο γάρ οἱ ζῆν πολὺ βέλτερον ἢ καὶ ἁπάσης
ἀγλαΐης ταρφθῆναι ἐν ἀσφοδελῷ λειμῶνι·
δὴ τότ' ἄρ' οὖν ἤμυσε κάρη πάλιν· αἶψα δ' ἔπειτα
ἐν δνοφεροῖς θαλάμοις κλαυθμὸς πολύδακρυς ὀρώρει·
κλαυθμοῦ δ' ἦ μάλ' ἄφωνος ἔησθα τότ', 'Αρτεμιδώρη.

m

XIII.

BACK TO BABEL.

I FORGET, for the moment—and perhaps I never knew—the exact date of the simultaneous emigrations from Babel. I think there must have been many grammarians that carried hods up the spirals of that never-finished tower. And I imagine they must have contracted a more than ordinary share of dizziness at the summit, and descended to transmit vertigo to all succeeding generations.

I have had on three occasions to march through Coventry with a little regiment of Latin and Greek tyros. Oftentimes, while jogging on at their head over a dreary common, I have Quixotically attacked grammatical windmills, under the conviction that their sails were going *whirr-whirr* to the grinding of no corn.

After laying it down as an initiatory dogma, that the two classical languages are sisters of our own good Saxon mother, I have often found it difficult to prove to my young disciples that their linguistic aunts are sisters of one another. To instance one difficulty that faces us at the outset. Their nouns are stretched upon diverse skeletons. The sides of Latin are furnished with six case-ribs, and those of Greek with but five. This would seem to indicate a difference of sex, and an Adam-and-Eve relationship. Was it in the Ante-Deucalion days, when Greek was fast asleep, that the rib was removed from his flank along Epirus?

The genitive case in Greek is made to do the entire work of the genitive and some work of the ablative of Latin; the dative of the former, the entire work of the dative and another part of that of the ablative in the latter; and many syntax rules of Latin seem to allow an unreasonable choice between the genitive and ablative. The rules for the gerund are ludicrous enough; but in that for the locative case we reach the acmè of grammatical unreason: —

In or at a place is put in the genitive case, if the noun be of the first or second declension, and of the singular number; but in the ablative case, if the noun be of the third declension, or if it be a plural noun of any declension.

Now, if this rule were correct in substance, it would seem to indicate as much coherence in Latin syntax as in the dreams of a maniac. After swallowing such a bolus of indigestibility, we might safely bolt anything: brace-buttons, tee-totums, corkscrews. I venture to suggest some analogues:

An active-transitive verb governs an accusative case, if the verb be of the first conjugation, and the noun of the fourth declension and of the feminine gender; otherwise, the verb may govern any case or no case, as you please.

An adjective agrees with its noun in gender, number, and case; excepting in the case of feminine nouns defective in the singular, and irregular in their habits.

I have an idea of publishing a cookery book upon the same principles of unreason. The following recipe I quote as an anticipatory advertisement: —

To make an apple-pie, you will compose the interior of currant-jam, if the pie be made on Wednesday, and the weather out-of-doors be windy; but of soap-suds, if it be your washing day, and the dish be of the willow pattern.

However, Reader, the fault is ascribable not to Latin, but to the exponents of its grammar. *In* or *at* a place, of course, was never, even in the Cannibal Islands, expressed by case-endings in so arbitrary a way. Such a locative rule would be lumbersome, if it were true; but, as you are aware, Reader, it is a tissue of nonsense from beginning to end.

I have an idea that some extra confusion was caused by the introduction of *the ablative case* into Latin grammar. And yet one should deal cautiously with a case that was begotten of the first and greatest of the Cæsars. There had been Dictators before Julius; but never an one with so catholic a spirit of autocracy. Like a steam-hammer, he could flatten a ball of metal, or settle daintily on an egg; and took an imperial part in the declension of his country's liberties, aristocracy, adjectives, and nouns. . The tyranny of an emperor, however, was usually limited in action to a select few. It was a perquisite of noblesse. I think it was so with the blunder of the ablative. I do not suppose any tradesmen, excepting those who served the Court, would take kindly to the bad grammar of the upper circles.

Half, if not all, the absurdities in our grammars arise from the fact, that the rules ·were enunciated when the theory of language was imperfectly understood, and when the two great languages were considered as alien to one another. Now, that we allow them to be kindred dialects of one great Arian form of speech, why should not a brief and simple and cheap manual be presented to young students, such as should bring out in clear relief so interesting a fact?

For my own part I am conscious of possessing one qualification for the task of writing one; the directness and plainness of speech that characterize my countrymen. But here my fitness ends. I have, indeed, studied some six modern languages, with a view of generalizing linguistic rules; but, I must confess, in a desultory way, and chiefly for my own amusement. I feel the poverty of my resources, and fear the light of intuition and of desultory study might prove a Will-o'-the-wisp. I have all the courage for the task, but lack breadth of philology. I fear those who are gifted with the latter will lack the former. It is so difficult to prove to such men that their linguistic knowledge has come in spite of an early training that has plunged nine-tenths of their school-comrades in an eternal Latin-and-Greek night.

Let us, then, borrow a Hercules from Germany; and having solemnly bound him over to an un-German brevity in the operation, send him with mop and broom and pail into the Augean stables, to cleanse them of their grammatical litter.

I venture, meanwhile, to suggest a case-classification of my own; partly for my own amusement in the building, and partly for the amusement of those who enjoy having something to demolish.

Præpositive	=	Nominative;
Appositive	=	Accusative;
Directive	=	Dative;
Possessive	=	Genitive in *s*;
Definitive	=	Genitive in a vowel.

1.

Præp.	*forma*	μόρφη
App.	*forman*	μόρφην
Dir.	*formaï*	μόρφηι
Poss.	——	μόρφης
Def.	*formaë*	——

2.

Præp.	*nautas*	ναύτης
App.	*nautan*	ναύτην
Dir.	*nautaï*	ναύτηι
Poss.	——	——
Def.	*nautaë*	ναύταο

3.

Præp.	*dies*	Σωκράτης
App.	*dien*	Σωκράτην
Dir.	*dieï*	Σωκράτεϊ
Poss.	——	Σωκράτεος
Def.	*dieë*	——

4.

Præp.	*navis, navs*	ὄφις
App.	*navin*	ὄφιν
Dir.	*naviï*	ὄφιϊ
Poss.	*navios, navis*	ὄφιος
Def.	——	——

5.

Præp.	*Deos*	Θεὸς
App.	*Deon*	Θεὸν
Dir.	*Deoï*	Θεΰ
Poss.	——	——
Def.	*Deoë*	Θεόë

6.

Præp.	*alius, allos*	ἄλλος
App.	*alium, allon*	ἄλλον
Dir.	*alii, alloï*	ἄλλοï
Poss.	*alius, alloïs*	——
Def.	——	ἄλλοë

7.

Præp.	*currus*	βότρυς
App.	*currun*	βότρυν
Dir.	*currui*	βότρυι
Poss.	*curruos*	βότρυος
Def.	——	——

8.

Præp.	*peds*	πὸςς
App.	*pedn*	πὸδν
Dir.	*pedi*	ποδι
Poss.	*pedis*	ποδὸς
Def.	——	——

The names of the first four cases of my system speak plainly enough for themselves. The fifth presents a little difficulty.

I may as well premise that only a noun can correctly be said to have a case or *relative ending.* An adjective and a participle may musically imitate a noun ; but strictly speaking they can only be said to have *cases of their own,* when they are used *as nouns.* In conversation a final consonant was continually dropped ; especially a nasal one, as *m* or *n.* This would be more often the case with the adjective or participle, when used as mere epithet, than with noun or verb, as they would, in most instances, immediately precede their noun, and the termination of the latter would sufficiently determine the case of both. The noun and verb would also drop their final consonant, when from position they could do so euphoniously and without causing ambiguity.

The Prepositive case is the shadow thrown in front by a coming verb. It is the forerunner of the king of the sentence ; a grammatical gold-stick. Its termination was, perhaps, originally the letter *s ;* which may possibly be a corruption of the verb *asen* of existence.

The Appositive is a page that follows close upon its king, holding up his train. It follows a verb of *action* or *motion*. All verbs of action are transitive. An active-intransitive verb would be a horse-marine in grammar or in common sense. An appositive would follow *abire* even more naturally than it would follow *amare;* as the physical motion of the former verb is more easily grasped than the mental or spiritual motion of the latter. Consequently, if a special rule were required at all, it would be required rather to explain *amat patrem* than *abiit domum.* The final *m* or *n*, which was often used separately as a preposition in the forms of ἀνὰ, ἐν, εἰς, or ἐνς, *in*, probably *ins*, and of our own *on*, was possibly the root or infinitive of a verb signifying *to flow* or *move.* We may detect this verb in Ὠκεανὸς, *annus*, *amnis* or *annis*, *Aniens, Evenus, Simoents*, *no*, *anats*, ἀέναος; in ἱστάναι, τιθέναι, διδόναι, ζευγνύναι, τύπτειν; in the old Latin infinitives *amaën, moneën, audiën, gnoën, soluën, regen;* in τύψαντος, τιθέντος, τύπτοντος, ζεύγνυντος; in *amantis, monentis;* in participial nouns as *dente, monte;* in the Latin infinitives when they pass into the form of verbal nouns or *active* verbal adjectives, as *amandum, monendum, amandus, monendus;* in ous own Teutonic, *kommen, essen;* in *reading, writing,* or the more archaic *readend, writend.* In translating *ista domus est vendenda* by *yon house is selling* or *to sell,* we see how the *end* of Latin and the *ing* of Saxon is rendered by the preposition of motion *to.* We may as well observe that *ista domus est ad vendendum* or *ad venden* is older and correcter Latin than *ista domus est vendenda,* where music has changed *ad venden* or *da venden* into a verbal adjective corresponding to our *selling* or *saleable.*

The Directive case is a sort of city-marshal, that orders rightly a procession. Its termination *i* is a modification of the word that terminates the Appositive, and particularizes, in the way of *in, at, on,* or *upon,* the action of some previous word, usually of motion, but not so necessarily; as, *dedit mihi; Carthagini restabat; utilis urbi; in*

oppido ; cum exercitu. Wherever I find a
noun attached to *in* or *cum*, I am very much
inclined to think we at one time had no
case at all; and, I am convinced that, if
fashion introduced a superfluous case-ending, it was the directive or dative.

The Possessive case denotes *ownership* or
possession; and, of course, it must either
have a noun clinging to it, or it must cling
to another noun, as a sort of barnacle or
parasite. It invariably ends in *s*, and has
a provoking tendency to turn adjective, and
imitate the noun to which it is attached.
In such words as *patris, militis, ejus, illius,
alterius,* it is content to remain unalterable :
in *cujus* it is apt to let music turn its head,
as in *cuja puella est, cujum filium vidisti ;*
though, one would think, *cujus* had no more
business to decline itself than its synonym
whose : as for *meus, tuus, suus, ἐμός, σός, ἑός,*
they have totally forgotten their noun-ori-
gin. I may as well state my suspicion that
*the adjectival use was possibly the first use of
all possessives.* If so, *cuja puella* is more correct than *cujus puella ;* and *patris, militis* deserve a declension as much as *tuus* and *suus.*

And now, not without fear and trembling, I proceed to treat of the Definitive ; remembering the trible warning—Be bold : Evermore be bold : Be not too bold.

The Definitive case was that case which enabled one noun, when applied to another, to *define, qualify, limit, specialize* or *particularize* this latter noun in almost every way EXCEPT POSSESSION. Its termination was probably a corruption of a preposition answering to *ἀπὸ, abs, ab ; eks, ek, ef ; von ; of.*

It would seem to be with case-endings as with theological disputants. If the latter differ *toto cœlo* from one another, there is room, perhaps, for mutual forbearance : if they overlap each other in doctrine, there is war to the knife ; as between men that jostle one another on the road to heaven. So is it with the Definitive and Possessive. They appear to have been quite unable to live at peace in any one noun together. Whichever of the two cases in any particular noun were the oftener needed, would gradually usurp the duties of the other. The Definitive, in Latin, is exiled from the

declensions of *u* and of *consonants;* or, if it
appears at all, is dogged by an adjective :
the possessive is extinct in the declensions
of *a* and *e;* and in the *o* declension, lingers
in the back settlements of *ille, qui, is, ipse,
unus, totus, alius,* and *alter.* This civil strife
of grammar-kinsmen has proved a Kilkenny
warfare in the end; for both cases have
disappeared from modern Italian, French,
Spanish, and Portuguese.

The disagreements of these cases led to
grammatical *mésalliances* at times. Thus
in such sentences as *filius erat* BONI PATRIS;
pater erat EXCELLENTIS VIRI; we have a
definitive adjective united to a possessive
noun, and a possessive adjective to a definitive. It is wrong in grammar, but what
can you do? *bonus* has lost its possessive,
and *pater* its definitive. It is ridiculous
to be always quarrelling. A compromise
is requisite for mutual preservation. So,
in Indian warfare, the Ojibbeway widower,
Bald-eagle, scalps the Great Snake, a Bene-
dict of the Mingoes; but falling a prisoner
into Mingo hands, is permitted to assume
the name and dignity of the dead hero:

with the wig of the departed dangling from his *châtellaine*, he takes possession of a cuckoo-wigwam, and comforts a not uncomfortable widow.

I have given, as the only specimens of surviving definitives, *nautaë*, *dieë*, *deoë*. We do meet with a few others, as in an occasional *neuter* of the fourth or *u* declension, where we detect the case by the adjective attached; and in a proper name, as *Ulyxei*. But we shall confine our attention to such ordinary instances as the three above. Their probable dialectic changes would be :—

nautavs	dominovs	dievs
nautav	dominov	diev
nautau	dominou	dieu
nautao	dominoë	*dieï*
nautaü	dominoi	*diê*
nautæ	*diminî*	
nautâ	*diminô*	

They would be *invariably attached to another noun*, and never governed by a verb. In such a sentence as *hoc non boni viri est*, *boni viri* is governed by a noun, that is so obviously implied in *est* as to be omitted

without risk of ambiguity. The case was
strictly *definitive* or *qualitative* in its operation; and is correctly used in such sentences as the following:—

> Erat homo magni ingenî;
> Erat homo magno ingenio;
> Erat matrona præclaræ formæ;
> Erat matrona præclarâ formâ;
> Erat animal permiræ specieï;
> Erat animal permirâ speciê;
> Erat tibia recurvi cornu;
> Erat tibia recurvo cornu;
> Erat filius honesti viri;
> Erat filia honestæ matronæ:

in the two latter sentences the Definitive
meaning appears to approach the Possessive: it certainly does not reach it.

In the following sentences we have specimens of fashionable, ordinary but incorrect
Latinity:

> Erat filius *sapientis viri;*
> Erat filia *prudentis matronæ;*
> Erat vir *ingenuæ indolis;*
> Finis erat *morientis dieï.*

Now, as the meaning of the Definitive
was so very apt to clash with that of the

Possessive, it is very probable that wherever it was resolved into two different forms, such as *nautæ, nautâ; domini, domino; diei, diê;* that for convenience and perspicuity, one form would monopolize the meaning of the dispossessed Possessive, although both might retain the original Definitive signification; thus we should use only *domini* for a possessive, but either *ingenî* or *ingenio* in a qualitative expression.

In regard to this phenomenon of the disagreement between Possessive and Definitive, the classic languages differ only in degree from that of our own Teutonic. Theoretically, all our nouns have a possessive; but practically only a certain number of nouns require them. The nouns, *table, piano-forte*, and *side-board*, would seem to merit a possessive as well as the nouns, *man, boy*, and *dog;* but while we should say, *a man's hat, a boy's cap, a dog's tail;* we should say, *the leg of a table, the tone of a piano-forte, the price of a side-board.* That is to say, the idea of possession chimes in easily with the meaning of some words, and not with that of others. These latter

words would be the first, then, to use a
definitive case to the exclusion of a possessive, even under those few chance circumstances where a possessive case might be
more appropriate. In course of time the
possessive endings for such nouns, from de-
suetude, would sound barbarous or pedantic : they would therefore be dropped altogether. Gradually, the *gramma of analogy, imitation, or fashion* would exclude the
possessive case for *similarly-sounding* nouns,
that really were in continual need of them ;
as it appears to have fared with *Dominus;
puer:* ἄλλος *;* Θεός.

At first sight, we should be inclined to
consider a Possessive case as a very marked
one in its signification, and one deserving
of special conservation. It has been, however, very scurvily treated. Greek and
Teutonic have dealt the most kindly with
it. Latin was moving in the direction of its
obliteration. Its place of refuge was in
the third and fourth declensions, as the declensions are badly named in our ordinary
grammars. The daughters of Latin have
condemned it, most unreasonably, to per-

petual banishment from France and the great southern peninsulas.

The Possessive has been well preserved in Teutonic dialects; as also in the granite-strata of Latin and Greek consonantal nouns. Our own Saxon is, in fact, a far older form of speech than the Greek of Homer. The Greek wore once the kingly crown of music, but surrendered it to the Italian, who wears it still. But the German, or, more correctly speaking, the Teuton-Hebrew, is now the emperor of instrumental sounds. However, the grimness of the old Teuton-pure lingers still in the final consonants of his language. Such words as *puela, pucrula, die, navi, ἄνθρωπο, ἄστυ* are not primitive: their terminations are the children of civilization. The words of old were *gwelas, gwerulas, dags, navs, ἄνεροψ, στάτς,* which rude forms were softened by the worshippers of a God of many names. Call him Sunlight; Music; Wine; Joy; Bacchus; Mercurius; Apollo. For Apollo took away the rude consonantal bagpipes of language, and replaced them with a flute of five stops, and gave the latter to the dwellers in

the Sea of Islands; to a race that loved music
and dancing. For the vowels are the music
and the light and wine and joy of language:
the notes of the human flute, which instrument, when breathed upon by love through
the lips of Youth and Maiden, is more
thrilling than the song of matin-bird, more
subtle-sweet than the even-song of nightin-
gale, more ravishing than the strains of
Israfel that hold the Angels mute.

We may trace the chain of ideas which
would lead to the extinction of a possessive
case in one language, or of a definitive in
another. Supposing I were to land on an
unknown island, and find a race of men
with something like a caudal appendage, I
should probably tell my friends, on my
return home, that I had seen a tribe of men
who wore *monkeys' tails.* And I should
be understood, although my grammar were
incorrect: I should have said, *the tails of
monkeys.* For a man may wear *a monkey's
tail,* of which he has deprived some unfortunate and surviving monkey, and may
wear it round his neck, or he may carry
it attached to him as a watch-guard, or

as a novel stimulant for educational purposes. But a man who wears *the tail of a
monkey*, or *the tail of the monkey*, will be
wearing it as his own tail; only, that the
appearance of it will suggest the idea of
that kind of tail, which at once *proceeds
from, or is connected with, or is defined,
specified, limited, or particularized by* our
ordinary ideas of a monkey.

Again; any butcher's boy may raise your
laughter by attaching a tin-kettle to *a dog's
tail;* but only a man of fine genius can draw
your tears by tying pathos to *the tale of a
dog.* A man, also, may be supported on
asses' milk; but he can only be said, correctly, to have *the brains of an ass.* There may
be special cases, however, where the use of
the possessive in the latter phrase may appear the more correct.

Let us now proceed to a brief treatment
of the Plural Number:—

1.

Præp.	*nautaï*	ναῦται
App.	*nautans*	ναύτανς
Dir.	*nautaïs*	ναύταΐς
Poss.	——	——
Def.	*nautaion*	ναυτάων

2.

Præp.	*Deoi*	Θεοί
App.	*Deons*	Θεὸνς
Dir.	*Deoïs*	Θεὑῖς
Poss.	——	——
Def.	*Deoion*	Θεῶν

3.

Præp.	*navies*	ὄφιες
App.	*navins*	ὄφινς
Dir.	*naviis*	ὄφιις
Poss.	——	——
Def.	*naviesn*	ὀφίων

4.

Præp.	*pedes*	πόδες
App.	*pedns*	πὸδνς
Dir.	*pediis*	ποδιις
Poss.	——	——
Def.	*pedesn*	ποδῶν

The real, and perhaps the only, pural letter is *s*. Those prepositives plural would gradually assume a vowel-ending, where the addition of an *s* to the prepositive singular would be sounded with difficulty, or would lead to a confusion with other cases.

The formation of the appositives plural is plain enough. I may as well state that such an appositive singular, as πόδα, has merely dropped its final nasal consonant ν; and that, probably, *pedem* dropped its *m* as often.

In the directives plural, a *b* or *v* would continually intrude, as in *pedibus, hominibus nobis, vobis:* in Greek, euphony was occasionally preserved by transposition, as in ὄφεσι or ὄφισι for ὄφις.

There are *no such cases* as possessives plural; for a very simple reason. We should have had to form them by the addition of a plural *s* to a possessive *s*, and they would have sounded very harshly to musical ears. I may as well say that possessives plural are very rare even in our own language.

The definitives plural are, perhaps, more puzzling than their singular correlatives. I believe they are nothing more than undeclinable adjectives, like what I suspected *patris, militis* to be. They are formed by adding *ov* or *en* to the prepositive plural. In such a word as *illorum*, the *r*, softly pronounced, is interchangeable with

i; as in *legitur,* λέγεται; and we can now perhaps, account for the anomalous accentuation of such a word as the latter on the grounds that the final syllable ται is not a diphthong but a corruption, probable of ταϱ. or τοϱ; as also for the accentuation of ἄνθϱωποι, and the like; and, reversely, for that of optatives where an οι *does* represent a diphthongal sound. The *r* intrudes, euphoniously, in *amare;* or it may replace an *s.* As we say in provincial English, *this is not of yourn,* so in old Latin they would say, *hoc non est vostri,* or *hoc non est di vostrn.* However, in *vostrn* we are startled with the appearance of a *t.* The word should have been *vosrn* for *vosn.* The termination is the same as that of *mine, thine, unsern, sein;* and of *yourn, hisn, theirn,* which, in the predicate, are more correct forms than *yours, his, theirs.* Perhaps the Spanish *vosotros,* and the French *vous autres* will illustrate the anomalous spelling of *vostrûm, nostrûm.*

Indeed, wherever I see the termination *ter* or *tr,* I suspect an idea of *otherty,* or the suggestion of a correlate; as in *nostr, vostr;* ἡμετεϱ, ὑμετεϱ; *either, neither; uter; alter;*

σοφωτερ; *better; magior* or *major; fa-ther, mo-ther; bro-ther, sis-ter; ma-ter-ter-a;* and *daugh-ter,* whose correlative is obvious in meaning, but lost in language.

Let us recur to *illorum.* Have you ever heard a Welshman, Reader, speak the word *Llangollen?* The sound of the double *l* is a sort of compromise between a whistling and a spitting. I could express it on paper with a pen that spluttered. Remembering this, we may follow *illorum* through strange windings; thus: *illoion, illôn, illorn, llorn, thlorn, thiorn, theirn, their.* So *aliorum* would suggest ἄλλοιον, used indeclinably; and *eorum* the Teutonic *ihren.* And *aliarum* or ἄλλαιον is more correctly used than ἄλλοιον, in speaking of women. And *alienus* is a declinable form of them all, and is in-correctly formed as having one termination appended in two ways. The termination *on* or *en* or *n* was, I believe, recurred to in Semitic or Arian languages, to form such words as were not worth the trouble of de-clining, under which category would come all neuter nouns, and neuter adjectival forms, that might be used as definitives plural or dual. Indeed, I imagine that the greater part of Greek dual words would disappear before a strict scrutiny; and that such words as *twain, kine, oxen,* are not duals or plurals, but adjectival words used in an indefinite and somewhat lazy manner. And I also imagine that the *n* of third persons plural is grammatically incorrect, but lazily convenient. Am I in earnest, Reader, or simply havering? Have I made some curious discoveries? or, what is more probable, some curious blunders? Have I sprung a mine of philology, or sprung a leak? The issue either way will serve to point a moral: will encourage or deter, by demonstrating the advantage, or the danger, of trusting to mother-wit.

I now proceed to treat of classes of words not included in my case system, such as *patre, milite, prudente; domine, asine.* These are respectively termed in our Grammars Ablative and Vocative cases. I assert that they are not cases at all; that the so-called Ablatives above given are only crude forms or Name-words; and that such Vocatives as *domine* have merely exchanged a short *o* into a short *e*, from the fact that a short *e* is the shortest of all vowel sounds.

In such sentences as —

> Ibat *trans pontem :*
> Ibat *per urbem :*
> Ibat *contrà murum :*

we have the appositive *pontem, urbem, murum,* correctly attached to the transitive words *trans, per, contrà,* which are corruptions of participles, or of similar words used absolutely. But in such a sentence as —

> Ibat *in Siciliam,*

we have the preposition *in* superfluously prefixed to *Siciliam,* according to the grammar of analogy and imitation.

In such sentences as —

> Turba ruit *ex oppidō :*
> Id dixi *de puerō tuō :*

I consider that the words *oppido* and *puero* admit of two explanations. If their final vowels be really long, then they are definitives, and the prepositions *de* and *ex* are usefully, but somewhat incorrectly prefixed. I am inclined, however, to think that the words are really only crude forms, or name-

words, and that their final vowels should
be short. The final vowels of name-words,
being often the same as those of corrupt
forms of the definitive cases, might possibly
usurp the pronunciation of the final vowels
of these latter, which are properly long as
being contractions. Or, perhaps, the ambiguity would be confined to reading; as in
spoken Latin we should pronounce the *o* in a
name-word like the *o* in *cot, lot, martello;*
and the long *o* of a definitive like the *o* in
wrote, smote, bocca: the *o* in *cosa* being different from both as representing the diphthong *au.* At all events, I am convinced
that, in familiar speech at least, the ancient
Latins would continually prefix prepositions to forms crude in such expressions as:—

> Id dixi *de tuŏ patre:*
> Non erat *in totă urbe:*
> Saxum ruit *de summŏ monte:*
> Id feci *clàm meŏ patre et tuă matre.*

With regard to what are called Ablatives
Absolute in Latin and Genitives Absolute
in Greek, I am convinced that originally
and correctly we should have no case at all.
A case is a *relative termination,* implying

something that has preceded or something
to follow.　If so, an absolute case is a con-
tradiction in terms.　In absolute or independent expressions, only name-words or crude
forms should be used.　I have already observed that many name-words would be
easily confounded with definitive cases; and
definitive cases are continually confounded
with possessive cases; consequently, a name-
word might in an absolute expression in
Greek be occasionally but incorrectly replaced by words really possessive.　We
must not forget, also, that a possessive case
is possibly an adjectival word in disguise.

I conclude with the consideration of some
peculiar expressions.　In the following:

> Vir erat *excellenti ingenio;*
> Vir erat *præstanti sapientia;*

the words in italics may be considered as
definitives; and, if so, their final vowels are
long.　But I think it would be correct
familiar Latin to say —

> Uomo erat *eccellentĕ ingeniŏ;*
> Uomo erat *præstantĕ sapienză;*

and that here the words in italics are name-words or crude forms, and that a preposition such as *de* or *di* is omitted, as in such a German sentence as :—

Geben sie mir ein *Glas-wein ;*

where *von* is omitted, as being clearly implied.

In other words, I am convinced that we have pure conversational Latin, such as Virgil may have heard in his nursery by the Mincio, in such modern sounds as—

Uomo erà di eccellente ingenio ;

Uomo erà di præstante sapienza ;

Meo' padre non è in casa ;

Tua figlia erà donnicilla di ammiravile venustà ;

Io e meo' fratellos eràmo moltò attoniti ;

Sì facta illa tua volontà ;

Eràno gioveni totò pieni di virtù.

I subjoin a pair of riddles, with one of which the future poet may be supposed to have puzzled his grandmother, and with the other to have made love for the first time to a young milliner of Mantua. The latter is in a rude dactylic measure; for Maronello is, of course, as yet unacquainted with the severities of scansion.

"Quid fâres," dissè puellulos porcello, "εi essem te." "Mâllem, m' ercule," respondè porcellos, "me esse te, quàm id esse, quod essem io, quodque esses tu." "Ah!" respondè puellulos, "si essem porcello', non essem porcello'."

> O mea bellula, cara Puellula,
> In meo pectore quod micat, Primulom
>   Est et erit tui plenom amore :
> O si calfâr' io Primuli ignibus
> Illud Sequundulom, quod gremi' in tuo
>   Urit me frigidiore nitore !
> Dom mea carmina vesperi perlegis,
> Mal' ominato' ne Totulom impleat
>   Crudelitate te meque dolore ;
> Sed te, Puellul', Amoris auccellula
> Prætrevolans tuom impleat gremiom
>   Debito tu' amatoris amore.

In some of which sentences, I have modified such words as *sapientia, est, dominicilla, venustate, sit, erant, pleni, dixit, ego, faceres dixit, respondit, avicellula, præter,* only in such ways as I see clearly indicated in my scanning of Plautus and Terence, and ratified by what I have read of Italian and Spanish; and I have made a free but Italian use of diminutives. The boy-poet's first riddle is easily solved; if a classical reader is puzzled with the second, he may go, for all I care, ἐς κόρακας.

Whatever may be the flaws in the case system of my suggesting, I can at all events explain to a young pupil the meaning of the terms employed, which I will defy any one to do with the terms *genitive, accusative, ablative.* If an inquisitive lad were to question me regarding the meaning of these words, or their fellow-inexplicables, *infinitive, gerund, supine,* and *participle,* I should say peremptorily: " Boy, you must call a gerund a gerund, as your father did before you." If he still asked me *why his father did so before him?* I should say humbly: " I don't know. They might have called a gerund a genitive, and a genitive a supine, and a supine a trumpeter. But they didn't."

You are tired, Reader, by this time. I can hear you somewhat indistinctly muttering: " Confound these cases: *do* let them alone." No: gentle but masculine Reader, it is just because these cases *are* confounded, that I am not for letting them alone. No; Reader: *me judice, illa antiqua vocabula non* CONFUNDENDA *sunt, quippe quæ jam satìs confusa sint; sed prorsùs et in æternum* DAMNANDA.

XIV.

DISSOLVING VIEWS.

Δός μοι ποῦ στῶ, καὶ τὴν γῆν κινήσω,
said Archimedes, as I once read in my Greek
Delectus; and it was a very hard sentence
to parse. Luckily for us he never obtained
his stand-point, or, heaven knows, we might
now be rolling on the far side of Uranus.
I am inclined to think, that, if a stand-point
be requisite, it will be as hard to move an
orange as a world. For a stand-point denotes rest; and rest, I fear, is denied to
more than the wicked.

The Hebrews have only a Future and a
Past Tense; and by a slight modification
they can interchange these two. Why have
they no Present? We can hardly suppose
a tense more often needed than the latter.
It is possible that this curious gap in the
Hebrew verb was caused by a corresponding

gap in our intellectual condition. Let us consider whether those languages, with which we are familiar, are better provided with times or tenses than their far-off Semitic cousin.

The first verb to which I am introduced in a Greek grammar has the following tenses usually assigned to it:—

τύπτω, ἔτυπτον, τύψω, ἔτυψα, ἔτυπον, τέτυφα, τέτυπα, ἐτετύφειν, ἐτετύπειν.

Now, the root of the verb is obviously τυπ; our own *tap, dab, dub,* and *thump;* in the latter of which words the *m* is complemental to the *p,* as the *p* is complemental to the *m* in the name of the writer of this bookling. Consequently, in τύπτω, ἔτυπτον we have derivative forms, habitual or frequentative tenses. Of the original verb then we have only left us, —

τύψω, ἔτυψα, ἔτυπον, τέτυφα, τέτυπα, ἐτετύφειν, ἐτετύπειν.

In other words, we have only means left us of expressing future and past time.

Again; τύπτω, being a tense of habituality or frequentativeness cannot be a present tense; for the idea of the present is con-

nected with the idea of a point of time, and
the idea of habituality with duration.

Again; let me search the wished-for tense
through the Passive. In my grammar I find
the following tenses:—

τύπτομαι, ἐτυπτόμην, · τυφθήσομαι, τυπήσομαι,
τετύψομαι, ἐτύφθην, ἐτύπην, τέτυμμαι, ἐτετύμμην :

and, eliminating the tenses that are bur-
dened with the *τ* or *ετ* of habituality, I
have—

τυπήσομαι, τετύψομαι, ἐτύπην, τέτυμμαι, ἐτε-
τύμμην :

Futures, Past-futures, Pasts, Present-pasts,
Past-pasts—but no Present.

Let me search the Middle or Reflective
Voice.   I find:—

τύπτομαι, ἐιυπτόμην, τύψομαι, ἐτυψάμην, ἐτυ-
πόμην :

eliminating as before, I have for tenses of
the primitive verb, only

τύψομαι, ἐτυψάμην, ἐτυπόμην :

only Future and Past.   No Present.   The
dove has returned to the ark; but there is
no leaf in her bill, to tell of dry ground on
which the foot may rest.   Close the window; and let us sail on through the dark.

But, for a moment, Reader, let us return to examine our remnants of the Passive. We had left us,

τυπήσομαι, τετύψομαι, ἐτύπην, τέτυμμαι, ἐτε τύμμην ;

or in older forms :—

τυπ-εσομ-αι, τετυπ-εσομ-αι, ἐτυπ-εσαμ, τετυπ-ομαι, ἐτετυπ-ομην ;

or, in other dialectic forms : —

τυπ-εϱομ-αϱ, τετυπ-εϱομ-αϱ, ἐτυπ-εϱαμ, τετυπ-ομαϱ, ἐτετυπ-ομεϱαμ.

And in ομαϱ, ομεϱαμ, εϱομαϱ, I fancy I can detect reflective forms of εἰμὶ, ἦν, ἔσω; *som, esam, esom; sum, eram, erom.* If this be the case, my Passive Voice has dwindled down to one tense, ἐτύπην or ἐτύπεϱαμ ; and my passive can only express the Past.

And is this incapable of explanation? Not at all. The Passive Voice is seldom needed: when it is, the verb *to be* alone can help us. I should say of a man : *he* WAS *drowned*, if he were thrown overboard ; but, *he* GOT *drowned*, if he jumped overboard. And when a cowardly ruffian is brought to the Old Bailey, we should say of him, in the Middle or Reflective Voice, *he* GOT *hanged;*

which expression would imply, *And serve him right.* It is only a mawkish sentimentality and a sham philanthropy that would describe the circumstances in the Passive Voice. And let me here observe also, how ridiculous it is to tell a man to go and BE *hanged.* The man will tell you that such a result depends on others, not on himself. A *passive imperative* is a blunder in any language. For *be* substitute *get*, and the above command is grammatical and feasible.

Again : I can say of a man, with grammatical correctness, *he was hanged;* for both *was* and *hanged* are past. But if I say, *he is hanged;* while *is* seems present, *hanged* is undoubtedly past, so that I am using a Past-present. If I say, *he is being hanged,* I talk nonsense; for I am speaking of a man *being now in the past condition.* And if I say *he will be hanged*, I have here a future in *will be* and a past in the participle, so that I am using not a future but a Past-future. Our own passive, therefore, has only a Past, a Past-present, and a past-future, and cannot clearly express a pure Present or a pure Future.

But again; let us examine those terminations, ομαι, ομην, εσομαι. They are probably reflectives of εἰμὶ, ἦν, ἔσω; of which I here give possible dialectic varieties : —

εἰμὶ	ἦν	ἔσομ
εσμι	εσαμ	εσομ
ασμι	εσαμ	εσομ
ασομ	εσαμ	εσομ
asom	esam	esom
sum	eram	erom ;

where an attempt is made to express present, past, and future, by a vowel-play upon the root, *as*, *es*, or *is*, in combination with the objective case of the first pronoun. We shall return erelong to this mysterious verb of existence, which plays in so strange and pretty and subtle a way with the tripartite divisions of time.

But to return to my riddle of the Present. Surely if this time can be arrested at all, it will be so in the verbs *to be, to do, to have;* and I seem to have caught the shadow in such sentences as, *How* DO *you* DO? *I* AM *tolerably well.* J'AI *terriblement faim.* But neither health nor hunger are momentary.

They indicate conditions, and conditions imply duration. And when I read, *How* DOTH *the little busy bee improve* EACH *shining hour?* the word *each* makes of *doth* a tense of habituality, an indefinite, an Aorist. Another trial or two ere we give up in despair. *God* HAS *mercy upon all that turn to him.* Why, friend, this *has* is eternal, and embraces all the past and all the future. And *God* IS *good;* but I dare not limit the duration of this little *is.*

Again, when I say *Pater meus me amat,* I probably mean my father loves me *habitually,* not at this special moment more than at any previous one : if so, I am again using a frequentative tense, or an indefinite tense, or an Aorist tense ; which in plainest English may be called a *what-d'ye-may-call-it* tense. Now, the expression *My father does love me* is only a little more emphatic than *My father loves me;* and the emphasis is given by simply breaking up *loves* or *loveth* into its constituent parts, and inverting their order. Hence, if the one sentence refers not to present time specially, the other will not so either.

Shall I then be nearer the mark if I say
My father IS LOVING *me*. It certainly would
seem so at first sight. But, alas! while *is*
appears to repose in the present, loving is
saddled with a termination that suggests
motion, and this motion neutralizes immediately the previous suggestion of repose.

Let me now pull to pieces two tenses of
old Greek and new Romanic:—

τύψω	chanterai
τύψεις	chanteras
τύψει	chantera
τύψομεν	chanterons
τύψετε	chanterez
τύψουσι	chanteront ;

which in older forms would be—

τύπεσομ	chanteraveo
τύπεσες	chanteravsti
τύπεσετ	chanteravt
τυπέσομες	chanteravomes
τυπέσεσες	chanteravstis
τυπέσεντ	chanteravnt

Why dear me, Reader, I find my supposed
essentially present words, *am* and *have*, doing duty as Futures. They are Detective
Officers; Policemen in plain clothes.

Again; observe the following three tenses:

canom	canem	canam
canis	canes	canas
canit	canet	canat
canimus	canemos	canamos
canisis	canesis	canasis
canont,	canent,	canant :

These tenses are called respectively, the Present Indicative, the Future Indicative, and the Present Subjunctive. They are obviously modifications of one tense: which of the three is the primary one? If *canom;* then upon an indefinite foundation we build our tenses of futurity and dubitation. Most correctly. Were dubitation to rest on firmer ground, it would cease to be dubitation. Surely there is a Proteus in grammar as well as on the ribbed sea-sand: an Isis in every class-room, whose veil even a schoolmaster may not lift.

In Algebra, I speak of a man as possessing + two pennies or — two pennies; which expressions interpreted into common speech mean that the man has either twopence in his pocket, or owes twopence, which he will have to give up as soon as he gets that sum. But how can I grasp the idea of a man's having *no pennies?* how shall I illustrate his condition? The fact is, the instant the idea of a penny is presented to my mind, the idea of negation becomes impossible. What could a man do with *no pennies* or *nuppence?* Could he play heads or tails with it? or put it in the bank? or in the plate at church? He might swallow it, perhaps, without doing himself harm; or give it to a beggar, without doing him much good.

I have a dim idea that past tenses begin with negative infinity; and that future tenses end in positive infinity; and that the grammatical present is the mathematical zero.

Are you a little confused, Reader, with the apparent irrelevance of *Nuppence?* and *Present Time?* If you were the writer of this little book, you would know how closely connected were these intellectually-illusory, but practically-palpable ideas.

Well, Reader: 'tis a transitory world: let us eat and drink, for to-morrow we die. What says the Epicure? *Carpe diem: Enjoy the Present.* The Present? why, it is gone ere the word is uttered. How futile must be a moral bidding, that enjoins the performance of a grammatical impossibility!

But what says the Apostle? *Here have we no abiding city. We seek a country.* Yes, Friend, the Past is gone; the Present crumbles beneath our feet: the Future is a stern reality, and all else is dream.

We are indeed walking in a vain shadow. The inner spirit endeavors ineffectually to express her thoughts by Language, Music, and Painting. Homer, Mozart and Raffaelle spake her meaning with a superhuman clearness. But, after all, Language is but a subtle intermixture of four sounds; dental, palato-lingual, guttural, and vocalic; and even these have a tendency to interchange. Music is but an infinite modification of a few simple notes; and Painting but the skilful blending of a few simple colors. Could we resolve them into their elements, we should probably find they were three in one; and that the one was Silence, or a Still Small Voice.

So with the tripartite division of time: *asom, esam, esom:* one word but very slightly modified. Ah! Reader, the grand old Hebrews had a serious and subtle reason for not facing the riddle of the illusory Present. They knew it was an idea inconsistent with the transitoriness of human things. And therefore with them, God was the only and unpronounceable I AM; the great, eternal and only Present; embracing all Pasts and all Futures. He is, indeed, the Word, the Verbum; and there are parts of speech, his Ministers, that modify the relationship of us mortal Nouns to the one primary Verb. For we are all governed by Him. They say that some are forgotten of Him, given over utterly. It must be a terrible thing for a Noun to be in that Absolute Case.

It may be heterodox in me, Reader, but I cannot help thinking these poor Nouns are never wholly absolute or disconnected. I think there is some Preposition of Mercy latent or understood, that links them to the surrounding clause; which Preposition will be supplied and made apparent, when the MASTER comes to parse the ravelled sentence of circumstance.

XV.

THE KING OF THE ALPHABET.

THERE are three letters that play an imperial part in language, *P*, *K*, and *T;* but the greatest of these is *K.* Thought is the soul of the universe ; language is thought in action. Silent thought is electricity in abeyance. Our brains are charged batteries : our nerves are conductors : with the friction of circumstance the force explodes in the faint thunder of continuously-rolling words. *K*, then, is emperor of a dominion to which the realms of Alexander, Augustus, Charlemagne and Kubla-khan were, in compare, but the farms of bonnet-lairds. He is the Pluto of the alphabetic trio, and his dwelling is in the throat-caverns of humanity, where, as we shall see, he is conversant with toil and trouble and lamentation and pain.

In conversation once with my friend, the

Professor of Natural Philosophy in Dunedin University, I stated my conviction that it was possible to represent the vowels and the primary consonantal sounds musically, pictorially, and mathematically; by vibrations, drawn curves, or equations to curves. I also gave it as my opinion that we should probably find the vowels and liquid sounds represented by continuous vibrations or continuous curves; and discontinuous sounds by points or cusps, or those discontinuous curves which suddenly quit a plane, to reappear at a distance, like that runaway streamlet of Elis of which we read in old story-books.

He informed me that an ingenious philosopher had carried out my idea experimentally; had set a suspended needle vibrating to definitive sounds, while a sheet of sooted paper was being moved horizontally against the needle-point; and that the vibrating point had traced upon the sliding paper special curves for special letter-sounds. The *m*, for instance, was represented by a continuous wave, which, strange to say, was its original shape in the old Phœnician alphabet, as its name was the *wave-letter*. You will remember, Reader, how *m* or *n* enter into numerous terminations that convey the idea of motion. The letter *r* was found to be represented by a continued series of convex and concave lines, resembling the edge of a saw. I am convinced that such a sound as *mud* would be pictorially discontinuous; that every syllable ending with *m* or *n* or *l* or *r* would roll continuously; and that such a sound as *stick*, *kick*, or *peck*, would, if pronounced with Stentorian energy, make a hole in the experimental paper.

In almost every alphabet the letter *k* resembles a pole with an arrow-head or a wedge fixed in it. Passing from the roots of words to derivative forms, it is subject in all Arian languages to a great diversity of phonetic corruption. It changes into *c*, *ch*, *h*, *g*, *gh*, *y*, *wh*, *quh*, *qu*, *f*, *v*, *w*. In many very ancient roots it occurs, in its harshest forms, in combination with a simple vowel sound, and unaided by any other consonant. These roots will almost invariably be found to convey the cognate ideas of *sharp-pointedness*,

sharpness, pain, fixature and *conjuncture.*
It is the hook and eye of language; it is
reiterated in *hook,* and liquefied in *eye;* it
beads together sentences with *que* and *καὶ*
and *κε;* begins all relatives, as *qui* and *who*
and *ὅς* and *κεῖνος* and *yon;* and sticks, a
relative barnacle, on to *hic* and *nunc* and
tunc and *quisque* and *each;* is embedded in
this and *that* and *οὑτὸς;* is the substance of
the first pronoun; is present in the kindred
and antediluvian words *was* and *went;* is
the affix that gives his *rhetoric* to the .
orator, and her *music* to the Muse.

United with the letter *n* in the root of
a word, it will be found to convey the idea
of a *cusp* or *barb* or *angle;* and from thence
will flow rivers of words conveying cognate
notions of *difficulty, pressure, pain and
sorrow.* It is horribly obvious in *hanging,*
in whatever tongue you conduct the operation. And remember the shape of the
Roman yoke of shame, and our own gibbet.
The former was the upturned angle of a
k, and the latter is a *capital gamma.* How
ridiculous it would be to suspend a criminal
from a gallows shaped like a poplar! Why,

he would dangle like a minnow from a
fishing-rod, or a blot from a long *f* in round-
hand.

And while I am on this lugubrious theme,
let me draw attention to the ominous names
of *Cal*-craft and *Ketch*, which are obviously
corruptions of *Col*-craft and *Tchek*. Is it a
chance coincidence, that the root of the
former word is identical with that of *col-
lum*; and that of the latter with the root of
πνίγω, ἄγχω, *ango, hang, choke,* and *Thug?*

You will find the *kn* or *nk* or *gn* or *ng*,
or other varieties of this angular sound,
scattered over all the organs of the human
frame: which makes me think that the
words *chin, knail, knose, knee, ancle, gena,*
γένυς, *knuckle,* were originally applied only
to the ruder-shaped sex, and afterwards
transferred, incorrectly and impolitely, to
the sex whose form is a series of entrant
and re-entrant graceful curves. Observe the
statue of a Venus or a Hebe: you have the
deification of curvature: you marvel at
what Nature or Genius can effect with an
infinity of round or oval o's. But gaze
upon the man who is just stripped for bath-

ing in that exquisite Cuyp in our Dunedin gallery : he puts one leg in front of the other; he squares both arms preparatory to a dive; and the fellow is a dislocated *K*.

The consideration of this sexual difference of shape convinces me that men are but bodily consonants, and women spiritual vowels. Your vowel may give a flute-music by itself; but your consonant is dumb, unless quickened to sound by vowel inspiration. And this explains to me why no poet can sing a song worth hearing, no painter draw a face worth regarding, unless the tongue of the one, and the fingers of the latter move responsive to the influence of love; and also, how, in a celibate condition, women may be suggestive of beauty and music, while bachelors are but unsuggestive symbols of unpronounceable, dumb nothingness. In true and perfect wedlock the vowel should retain its music, and the consonant its directive force. Wherever this latter force is unsexed or vocalized by petticoat usurpation, there have we in married life a flabby symbol of the diphthong.

Again; the conjuncture of letters, *kn*,

conveys often the idea of connection; as ir con*j*uncture and con*n*ection, and *con* and ξὺν, and *link* and ζευγνύω: and the analogous idea of mental power; as in *ken*, *gnovi*, γνῶναι.

Unite the *k* or guttural with the liquid *r* or *l*, and you pass from the region of angles to that of curves; and you will usually find that *kr* will denote a short curve, or a rough sound; and *kl* a long, sweeping curve, or a reverberant and rolling sound. There are three horned animals; the *gnu*, the *cervus* or κέραος, and the *elk;* in whose respective names we have indicated the angular-sharpness, the curvilinearity, and the branching sweep of horns or antlers.

If you place a *p* before the *k*, you will come upon a host of words which all spring from the one idea of *sharp-pointedness.* And you will not often find a root to which you may attach every vowel sound in three languages, and detect through all phases the primary idea; as in *pack, peck, pike, poke, punch; pac-tum, pecten, pix, foc-us, pupug-i;* πάγ-ος, πηγ-νύω, πικ-ρός, ποκ-ος, πὺξ; where the vowels in turn amalgamate

with *p* and *k*, while the force of these latter
is distinctly marked in every word ; in the
crystallization that suggested πάγος and
πύξ ; in the pointed flames of the *focus* or
fuoco ; in the tangled πόχος, that suggested
the *pecten ;* in the flame-tapering shape of
the *pix,* or πεύχη, or *pikn,* or *pine.*

Again; if you put *p* after *k,* you will
. come upon the series of words of a very
different kind ; where the idea of *hollowing,*
or *scooping,* or *digging out* is discernible,
and the *shape* suggested is that of a *channel,*
or *bowl,* or *skull ;* as you may see in *curve,
grave, groove, cup, gulph, scoop, ship, shape,
schaffen ; caput, cavus, scapha ;* σχάπτειν,
γράφειν, γλύφειν.

Our *k* does not seem to agree very well
with *t.* If they go in pairs at all, the dental
is apt to struggle for precedence in place
and predominance in sound : under all circumstances he holds his own.

I have endeavored to show, then, that
there are a series of classes ; each class com-
prehending a very great number of words ;
of which classes—

One consists of words where *k,* or some

equivalent, is in combination only with a vowel;

A second of words, where *k* is in combination with the ringing nasal *n;*

A third, were *k* and *r* combined;

A fourth, where *k* and *l;*

A fifth, where *p* and *k;*

A sixth, where *k* and *p.*

It would thin a dictionary remarkably to remove from it every word that could be brought under one of the above six categories.   I should have no objection to such a removal, could we simultaneously remove all the pain and sorrow of which the guttural words are the exponents. Your Gaelic mountaineer and honest Teuton retain the guttural in all its pristine harshness. Your effeminate southern discards it; but there is as much of virulence in his *odiare*, that has lost his chief letter, as in the *hate* that has softened it, or the ἔχθος where it shows in force.

Our conversation, then, would be wonderfully limited, if the *k* or its equivalents were eliminated No wonder, you will say: for is not *k* the guttural; and is not the guttural

the specific sound of the throat, the channel-
pipe of all sounds? Of course it is, Reader,
and all our *k's*, and half our wickednesses
come out of it; and if they stuck there they
might choke us; and if they did, we might
be submitted to a post-mortem examination,
and the doctors would all agree that, in addition to the disobedience of our first parents, there had been a conspiracy of garot-
ting gutturals concerned in our *choking*.

But, Reader, I have hitherto amused myself, and perhaps wearied you, with discursive bantering upon a really solemn subject. All human knowledge, as you are
aware, was obtained by the sacrifice of im-
mortal simplicity. The letters of the alphabet are the elemental atoms of all language;
language is the poor human exponent of all
knowledge; and Solomon has told us—and
we might have learnt it without his telling
—that all knowledge is but vanity; that he
who gathereth knowledge, doth but garner
sorrow. For let the Sun shine ever so
brightly, he cannot pierce the darkness that
Sin has brought into the world; and let the
winds make ever so tuneful music, they

cannot drown that universal cry of pain which Death, who is the child of sin, wrings out of poor guilty Humanity, and poor innocent, dumb Beastdom.

And now, Reader, you are more than prepared for my concluding statement. It must be as obvious to you as to me that this horrible *K*, whose catholic angularity is at work in all our bodily *agues*, stomachic *acidities*, heart-*aches*, and soul-*agonies*; in the *canker*-worm of remorse; in the *ægritudo* of a body or a mind diseased; in the ἄχεα of the sorrowful; the ἕλκεα of the wounded; the κωκυτοί of the mourner; and the κακία of us all; is the stern ἀ*NAΓK*η of the Greek, and the *dura* NEK-*essitas* of the Roman; whom we vainly attempt to propitiate, by a change of gender and an irreverently-familiar epithet, in our soubriquet of OLD NICK.

XVI.

FALLACIES.

" THERE is nothing new under the sun," said Solomon; and his apophthegm was as old as the truth it embodied. "Our learning is but recollection," said Plato; and what a deal he must have known, ere his memory was dimmed by his humanity! "What hath been, is, and will be," said, or thought, Pythagoras; and the sentiment was as true and trite as that of King Solomon.

Wise men of old have given us the potted essence of sagacity, in small canisters, such as we may carry about with us, without trouble, to the Equator or either Pole. Alas! too often, in starting on our life-journey, we hamper ourselves with burdensome provisions, that are found in a green mould ere the journey is half over.

Keeping in view the maxims above quoted, and that of Plato in particular, let us review the several words that at various times have been adopted to define or specify the occupation of a school-master.

He may be called a *Teacher.* But the root of the verb *teach* is the middle syllable of the word in*di*cate; and he who teaches, merely points out this or that with his *digits, doigts,* or *toes;* and it is obvious that the objects, to which he points, must be extraneous to himself.

Or he may be said to be employed in the business of *instruction* or *edification.* But these are simple building terms; and no bricklayer can make a wall out of his own head, however thick that head may be.

Or, again, in old-fashioned speech, for which we have Old Testament authority, he may be said *to learn* his pupils this or that language or science. And herein I observe how directly vulgar speech goes to the bull's eye of truth. For the verb *learn* may be used in a sort of reflective sense; and a man, who teaches Latin to his pupils, may be said *to get them to learn* or *recollect Latin.*

I have known a teacher of French laugh most unphilosophically at a pupil — behind his back — for pronouncing *chien* like *cayenne*. But the boy was in the right. The substance of *chien* he had been familiar with from childhood in the shape of its English homonym, *hound:* it was only with its *accidents* that he was unacquainted. How on earth could he, as a reasonable being, guess that a nation, in pronouncing such a word, would insist upon mis-pronouncing the strong guttural *ch*, upon dropping the final *n*, and sounding the word as though there were a *g* a mile off? Depend upon it, any logical little fellow will pronounce the word *correctly*, until he learns from his instructor how unreasonable and incorrect are the rules of speech.

Again ; a teacher of Latin is apt to deal harshly with a novice who, in a catholic spirit, makes *bonus* agree with a single soldier in the nominative, or a dozen old women in the ablative. The fact is, the boy would be wrong if he did anything else at starting. He is unconsciously making an *improvement* in language, which we prac-

tical people in England made long ago; to which the French, Italians, and Spaniards have partially advanced; and towards which the Germans are progressing with the same rapidity that characterizes their diplomacy.

The logical and praiseworthy pupil is inculcating the absurdity of saying *one thing twice over.* " Why," he argues, " in the following sentence, *I am a sensible lad*, I am quite aware that *lad* is *nominative* and *singular* and *masculine*, and also *that a* and *sensible* are inseparably connected with it, from the mere meaning of the passage. Why then should I bother myself about their spelling, for the purpose of proving to myself by ocular means what I know by the inspiration of mother-wit ? "

Hereupon, the Master will say to the logical but troublesome student: " Sir, the people of ancient Italy, like many other ancient people, had very musical ears; and consequently, when words agreed together in sense, they wished them to agree in sound. Not that the latter agreement was absolutely requisite. It was probably a harmony that owed its origin to an aural civilization of music and speech, and its decay to an ocular civilization of logic and paper. Perhaps it was found troublesome, like the pretty prolixities of a rococo politeness, and the stately tediousness of the old minuet. But although this agreement of mere sound was not peremptorily requisite, it is valuable as a suggestion of perfect concord. Thus, in married life, it is not enough that husband and wife should agree in essentials. I have, indeed, read of a married pair finding it prudent and economical for one to lean to fat and the other to engross the lean. The one-ness of the motive might justify the diversity of habit. But the experiment was fraught with peril. I am of opinion that there is but little prospect of harmony being maintained, either in married life or in Latin,—or at all events, in the relations of master and pupil,—unless concord be preserved in the minutest particulars."

And the pupil will now reply: " Well, sir, there is much in what you say; consequently, after this, whatever vagaries a noun may take into its head, I'll take good care that the adjective shall follow the lead.

If *homo* chooses to whistle into a dative plural, *felix* also shall whistle like a mavis. But surely, sir, you are not going to hurt my hand, because the old Italians had such provokingly fine ears for music?"

And hereupon the Master will smile, and drop something back again into his pocket, and will think to himself: " Why, this young fellow knows as much as I do about the substantialities of noun and adjective; it is merely the accidents of their dress, or sound, or appearance, with which he is unacquainted."

Again; when a boy, apparently dull, has his first lesson in geometry, he reads that *a point has no parts and no magnitude.* Why, this is a definition that would apply to *a thought; a smell; the tail of a guinea-pig;* to *pigeon's milk; a mare's egg;* or to *nothing-at-all.* I am convinced that many a boy, apparently dull, would grasp the idea of a mathematical point, who could never catch the force of the above definition. He could easily understand that a solid body occupies space; that space is bounded by surfaces; that surfaces are bounded by

lines, that lines are bounded by points.
And thus, from an intuitive idea of bulk,
he is led to a mathematical conception of
surfaces, lines, and points, without the aid
of a single definition. To commence the
study of geometry with a novice by the
definition of a point, is like commencing a
series of anatomical lectures with an account
of our once cellular condition, or the biography of a polemical theologian with a definition of *his* Christian charity.

Again: to define a straight line as that
which lies evenly between its extreme points,
is to give a definition that still requires defining; for the word *evenly* seems to beg
the whole question at issue. I believe a
better definition of a straight line would be
that *it was a line not crooked ;* or, perhaps,
a better one still, that *a straight line is a
straight line.* And if I wished a child to
grasp the idea of a point, I should ask him
to think of the sharp end of a needle, with
his eyes shut; or of the respect paid to learning in Dunedin, with his eyes open; and to
aid him in grasping the idea of a straight
line, I should ask him again to shut his eyes,

and picture to himself an arrow so thin that he could shoot it through a window-pane without breaking it; or I should ask him to imagine the course which an ecclesiastic would take, if a bull were behind him or a bishropric in front.

In arguing once with a mathematician of eminence, I asserted that I would make clear and intelligible to any non-mathematical man of common sense any symbolical expression however complex; provided only that I clearly understood it myself. He desired me to make the experiment with the expression

$$a^0 = b^0 = c^0 = \&c. = x^0 = 1.$$

I did so in his presence, and was allowed to have carried my point. And the inference I wish to be drawn from this is simply: that mathematical symbols very often, like moral aphorisms, are but brief and convenient ways of putting universally-known truths.

A pupil often dislikes a master unreasonably in his youth, and eulogizes him as unreasonably in manhood. " Ah ! " says he, as he sips his wine; " what little knowledge

I have was all got from old So-and so." Of course, he does not mean any one else to believe what he does not believe himself: and what, indeed, is not true.

When the praises of some great scholar or mathematician are being rehearsed, you may hear a master say with a pardonable pride: " Ay; So-and-so was my pupil for many a year." And he believes in the inference of his words, and wishes you to believe in it too. He is perfectly honest; but his inference is not true for all that. It may be partially true: it may be wholly false.

Your bricklayer plods with trowel at the foundation of the column; and the crow builds its nest at the top, adorning the capital with natural bird-lime; and the bricklayer and the crow deserve equal credit for the pillar's aërial grace.

A very poor teacher and a poorer scholar was speaking in my presence of a Cambridge star. " He read with me," said he, " for six years together." And I thought to myself: " Had he read with you for twelve, he would still have been an excellent scholar."

I grant that a vigorous and energetic tutor may cram to almost any extent a youth, whose health is robust, and whose bent of intellect is very prosaic and very acquisitive. He may, with a tremendous effort, push him very near to a First Class at Oxford; with a great effort, he may push him into the First Class at Cambridge; with a prolonged, but not exhausting effort, he may push him one-third of the way up the list of Wranglers; he may without difficulty, but not without patience and a long course of *pâté-de-Strasbourg* feeding, make of his pupil a Mandarin of the Blue Button in our Chinese Examinations for India and the Civil Service. So in the pages of Theodore Hook have I read, how a dog-fancier prepared an often-stolen dog for diverse markets; how, by processes of rubbing, polishing, cutting, clipping and fattening, the chameleon-hound passed through various metempsychoses, as spaniel, greyhound, retriever, bull-terrier, and mastiff.

But with a youth of fine talents, and a love of knowledge for its own sweet sake, a master can only fire his ambition by his precepts and his example. He can no more digest his mental than his physical aliment.

Does a master ever meet with such a pupil? very, very rarely. And, indeed, if a boy be gifted with good natural parts, and inclined to follow knowledge for herself alone, his motives for study are nearly sure to be corrupted by the foolish but pardonable ambition of his parents or his schoolmaster. "How is it," says a father, "that my boy is so low down in his class?" "I think," said the master to an old pupil, "you need not read such and such a book, for it's sure not to *pay* in any examination."

However, if your genius is rare, I verily believe that your dunce is a Phœnix still more rare. Indeed, I have never met with an undoubted specimen of the *booby*. Perhaps, a physically-healthy booby is as great a rarity as a live Dodo. I have known many lads to be classified under the category; but, on investigation, I have always found that their training was at fault; that the gravelly part of their intelligence was being ploughed, and the loamy part left fallow.

It seems to me that, in his intellectual capacity, a teacher has to point out to his pupils a writing on the wall, to direct their gaze, and to throw a good light upon the inscription. It is possible that young eyes will decipher it more easily and correctly than he does himself.

But, though young eyes are sharp, young judgment is not very trustworthy. So a boy may draw a wrong inference from what, in one sense, he clearly apprehends. He can run at great speed; more quickly than a grown man. Then keep him on the right road. When he comes to where many ways meet, let him find signposts, with inscriptions clear and short and legible; and be very careful that the signboards point the right way.

I have known instances where these signboards were duly set up, but the boards were considerably larger than those we see on turnpikes, and the inscriptions so long and indistinct, that, long before they could be deciphered, it was time to go to bed.

You remember, Reader, how Diogenes, to be busy like the rest of his fellow-citizens, rolled his tub up and down the market-place. Now if he had rolled it up and down a back-alley, he would have done no harm; and it was certainly not his intention to do any good. But in the market-place, you may depend upon it, he was terribly in the way. There are a great many respectable men among ourselves, who, with the best of motives, are unconsciously imitating the ill-natured Cynic, and who pass their whole lives in rolling big, empty tubs up and down our most crowded thoroughfares.—Were you ever present, Reader, at a debate in either House of Parliament?—In a century or two, I am convinced, the policeman will be making these tub-rollers move on.

In all her works, Nature, who is the handmaid of God, is simple and direct. We have no well-authenticated instance of her tying knots for the mere amusement of unravelling them. Man, in the majority of his works, displays a love of intricacy and obstruction; and more so in mental operations than in handiwork. A carpenter comes provided only with tools for chiselling and planing, and never turns aside to sweep a chimney or whitewash a ceiling. A surgeon proceeds at once to the amputation of a wounded limb, and never thinks of commencing operations by making the wound worse. But a schoolmaster, in teaching a language to a young pupil, burdens his lessons with explanations that are infinitely more perplexing than their subject. Many a child would have found Latin easy and interesting, had we not been at such pains to make it difficult and dull.

Many a child would find the Lord's day a day of calm and happiness; would grow up in the belief that religion was a sweet and pleasant thing; that virtue was not a hardship; that vice was of itself detestable; and that God was far wiser than even his own father, and kinder than even his own mother,—but for those ingeniously obstructive means that divines have invented for the purpose of checking the spontaneous spirituality of children. A child is supposed to be religiously brought up, if his Sunday hours are choked with liturgies and collects and catechisms. He repeats definitions of doctrines that are beyond the comprehension of humanity. He is taught to regard as sinful, actions as extraneous to morality as the neighing of a horse. His duty to God is made obscure by the midnight of super-fluous words. His duty to his neighbor, that intuition or example would impercept-ibly have taught, is made odious by being communicated in a long and difficult for-mula, which he has to repeat like a parrot. He prattles innocently of so wonderful a doctrine as that of eternal salvation for the good: and there is no harm in that: and of so terrible an one as that of the eternal con-demnation of the wicked. But he is not told that the word *eternal* means *everlast-ing*, and that *everlasting* means *eternal;* and that the meaning of either word is as much beyond the comprehension of a Newton as it is beyond that of a theologian or a baboon.

While the jumbling of a child's mental and spiritual nature is the business of the schoolmaster and divine, the jumbling of the interests of manhood, social, commercial, and political, is the prerogative of the states-man. How many a petty kingdom would have risen long ago into wealth and importance, but for the obstructive ingenuity of its well-meaning but tub-rolling rulers !

In former days the Faculty of Medicine rolled a tub terrible as the car of Juggernaut. Charged with a deadly erudition, the professional healer passed a knee-breeched life doing all manner of mischief among the people. To many an one a weeping Martha might have said: "Sir, if thou hadst *not* been here, our brother had not died." But of late years an ebb-tide of repentance has happily set in, and the Faculty now set an example to other professions of a reverence for Nature and simplicity.

The combined effects of the jumbling system, as pursued by teacher, divine, and statesman, make of society an easy prey to that cormorant profession which thrives on the garbage of man's follies and vices. In whatever country the lawyer class is wealthy and powerful, we may be sure that the schoolmaster and the divine are there either wholly idle or mischievously active. For the lawyer is, as you are well aware, Reader, the very incarnation of the ——; but no: my chapter is on Fallacies, and would close most inappropriately with a truism.

XVII.

NURSERY REFORM.

I AM very fond of dogs. They are religious beasties: but idolaters; for they worship us. The old Egyptians worshipped them. The dogs have the better of it in the comparison. On week-days a dog may suggest morality and religious faith; but he has a painfully profane look on Sunday. Poor heathen brute: he should run into hiding-places on Saturday at midnight, as a ghost vanishes at cock-crowing.

I am equally fond of cats. But they are utterly devoid of religion: sleek epicures, that live only in the present. They may coil cosily into roley-poley cushions; wash daintily behind their ears; and drone their drowsy little humdrum fireside-hymns; but with the best of them there is a faint, lingering odor of Beelzebub.

I should not wonder if, on the other side of Styx, some faithful friend were to welcome me with the wagging of a shadowy tail, and the utterance of a thin and ineffectual bow-wow. But the boat of Charon will push a difficult furrow through innumerable bodies, brickbat-laden, of purrless, soul-less, dead-as-door-nail cats. Poor pussies!

But though I love these hairy favorites much, I love little children more. And I care not whether they be blonde or brown; clean or dirty; lordlings or chimney-sweepkins. Not a button. I would rather they were not too good; or goody. Let us have a little naughtiness, sprinkled in at intervals: it gives a flavor to the insipidity of vegetable innocence.

A Pharisee is not a pleasant object, be he clad in swallow-tails or cotton frock. And there is a social Pharisee as well as a religious one. Clean face and glossy curls must never frown upon little, smutty, streetling Publican. No, no: it is quite possible that this little sparrow-boy but rarely washes his face; more rarely says his prayers; and never blows his nose: which practices are

common with genteel canary-children. But
not a sparrow falleth to the ground without our Father. Let us all have a share of
natural commonness; of wholesome naughtiness; of clean dirt. Let us stand occasionally in the corner of repentance; "out-
side of all joy, like Neptune in the cold."
Then will we promise to be good; we will
throw tiny arms half round papa's neck,
will kiss him half-way through his yellow
beard; we'll be happy for ever, and ever,
and ever, and live on toffey and almond-
rock. O the bliss of making up! The rain
after drought! the sunshine after rain!
Yea: 'tis a sweet thing and a pleasant to
have been a little naughty.

Eliminate misdoing from the world, and
you annihilate charity. The air is unin-
habitable from a surplus of oxygen. The
good deed shines no longer that glistened
like a glow-worm in a naughty world. Imagine, Reader, the humiliating condition of
a good parson who has overdone his duty;
the vestrymen are better than he; the clerk
is better than the vestrymen; the pew-
opener is suspected of being better than

them all. Why, the church is top-heavy:
another effort, and it will stand upon its
spire. Come back to the old ways, my
friend. There must be degrees: there must
be degrees.

But while I can regard with complacency
a little naughtiness in children, I am grieved
to the heart to see their eyes dimmed ever
so little, and their cheeks ever so slightly
pale. O me, for the faces that one sees at
times, so wee, and wan, and old! for the
little tiny Elders who begin life at the
wrong end!

I regret, also, that children are under
the absurd necessity of growing bigger; of
developing from baby-buds into boy tulips
and men-cabbages. They keep pet-spaniels
permanently small; but by means that
imperil their little lives. I wonder if an
elixir could be suggested that would keep a
child always a child. Nay: I know there
is such an elixir; and I know, also, from
what fountain it may be drawn; and has
been drawn. It is bitter, if you sip of it;
but sweet, they say, if you take a full quaff.
But he that drinks thereof cares not after-

wards for earthly meat or drink; but passes away, and leaves us; with a look of strange joy upon his countenance. And we follow him a little way, sorrowing. And I think he must wonder at our sorrow; and from under his green counterpane must hear, as from the depths of a sweet dream, our cry of *Vale! vale! in æternum vale!*

Did you ever sit, Reader, with your Babe upon your knee, and its dear, good Grandmother before you? Stretch out both hands, and you will touch very nearly at the zero and the infinity of life; the mystery of the forgotten Past, and the mystery of an unknown Future.

But to return to our dogs. I am glad that our homeless ones have found of late a genial and kindly advocate. But I could find it in my heart to deprive them of their patron; for to me they seem to be appropriating the children's bread; and I would employ his humor and his pathos to plead the more melancholy cause of our own poor, grammarless little ones. I would use all my eloquence to depict the miserable condition of these sweet victims of parental indifference : I would point to them, as they stood, blue and shivering, without a rag of syntax round their little loins; and show them dwining away before our eyes beneath the pitiless influences of grammatical destitution.

And moved by the eloquence of my pleading, and impressed with a conviction of its truth, some aged hosier in his latter days, ignoring the paltry claims of kindred, would leave a colossal fortune for the realization of my philanthropic schemes. And I should found a magnificent institution in the neighborhood of our Dunedin, and should call it the Caiêtêum, or the Normal Institution for the training of Nursery-maidens. And the building should be a palatial one, with green lawns and shrubberies and massive gateways; and there should be lodges at the gates, wherein should dwell porters, whose business it were at distant intervals to open and to shut those gates. And I would appoint a board of twenty Guardians, who should on stated occasions dine sumptuously out of its funds, for the benefit of the Caiêtêum. And I

would select a Governor of a grave and
dignified demeanor, and a numerous staff
of masters well skilled in the turning of
the gerund-stone. And from the Board of
Guardians should be selected a sub-com-
mittee of three members, who should be
named the Special Aggravators, and their
business it should be to worry the Governor
of grave demeanor, and to set the Governor
a-worrying the turners of the gerund-stone.
And the palace and the Board and the
staff, should be for the housing and the
superintending and the instructing of ten
little Nursery maidens, who should be
chosen exclusively from such families of
the name of *Thompson* as should spell it
with a *p*. And for a term of years these
little maidens should apply their noses to
the outer edge of the rapidly-turning gerund-
stone. And when their brains were cleared
of the weeds of nature, and mother-wit, and
unassisted sense, I should send them forth
as Missionaries into the outer world for the
reformation of our nurseries.

And wherever these little Missionaries
came, they would sweep away, as with a

besom, all idle games and silly puzzles and unedifying tales. And Jack would flee in terror to the summit of his own beanstalk; Cock-Robin would be borne unpitied to his grave; and Mother Hubbard, led by her own dog, would beg her bread, an exile in far distant lands. And our children should be instructed upon those scientific and theoretic principles, which in other and higher departments of education have stood the test of ages. And these Missionary-maidens should be furnished, each with her Gerund-stone; and resolute parents should apply the noses of their prattlers to the outer edge thereof, as it turned rapidly. But, forasmuch as the process might for a while prove disagreeable to the instructed, the Maidens should be further equipped with an implement of hardened leather, highly charged with a subtle electricity, whose dexterous application to the palm should have the property of endearing to the little ones these Maidens and their gerund-stones.

Follow me, gentle Reader, into a model Nursery, and behold our system in full operation. Those little children yonder, blue-eyed and flaxen-haired; fresh from the Eden, where innocents still wander; are standing for the first time before the mysterious engine of their mental training. From dawn to eve, this summer's day, they are committing to memory all words that end in *ock*, as *cock, knock, block, rock, stock, smock, flock:* beginning with a cock that must not crow: for the fowl is as yet unprovided with verb, and conjugation, and voice—most essential this for crowing—and mood and tense, and number and person: and ending with a flock that must neither frolic nor bleat. To-morrow they will give undivided attention to words that end in *dom*, as *kingdom, beadledom;* the day following, to words in *ition*, as *deglutition, perdition;* then to words in *ation*, as *trituration, botheration;* and so on for a month or two, till the category of ordinary words is exhausted. Then are they to be put to wholesome tribulation upon words that lack a singular, as, *tongs, scissors, spectacles, stockings, trousers, breeches;* then on nouns that lack a plural, as, *butter, beef, mutton, glue,*

alicompayne; then on nouns that lack a
possessive case, as *gruel, wash-hand-stand,
microcosm;* then on nouns that lack a vocative, as, *ninepins, oatmeal, cosmogony, philo-
progenitiveness.* And if, meanwhile, they
yawn over the work, or ask idle questions
of curiosity, they will be subjected to the
influence of the Electric Leather.

When sufficiently bewildered, it may be
irritated, with months of substantives, they
shall pass through similar ordeals of un-
diluted adjectives, participles, verbs, adverbs, numerals, prepositions, and conjunctions. Then shall they be put through a
course of syntax, which shall daily be ad-
ministered to them in infinitesimal doses,
according to the received principles of
grammatical Homœopathy.

Then shall be put into their tiny hands
the interesting and exhausting Biographies
of the great Busbequius Bungfungus; and
by homœopathic treatment each Biography
shall be made to occupy many weeks; so
that the children, in reading the death of
Palæologus and Mithrobarzanes, and other
favorite heroes, may have forgotten all the

circumstances of their lives. And if they read a fable, they shall read it in minute portions, so that, on arriving at the tail or moral, they may be unable to apply it to the body. And in their daily readings they shall continually sing their verbal and syntactic formulæ, which shall sound like mystic hymns in the ears of their delighted parents.

It is true that the children, by this method, will be powerless to express their passing thoughts, or to describe occurrences that take place before their eyes; but they will be imbued with theories of speech, too sacred to be employed in the profanities of idle talk; and for this their parents will feel duly grateful to the Leather of Electricity and the rapidly-turning Gerundstone.

But ah! Reader, all human devices are marred with imperfection. My own system, perfect as it may seem, is lop-sided, as it affects but the mental part of our nature. It is true, the lilies of the field toil not as they grow. The lambkin on the hill-side thrives pleasurably into sheephood: I wish

I could add, passes painlessly into mutton. The beaver learns his pontifical trade, un-stimulated by flaps of the parental tail. To the brain of man is decreed the proud pre-rogative of uncomfortable growth. No; not decreed : in this matter, I imagine, the sagacity of man has improved upon the wisdom of Omniscience.

The mental training of my own boyhood was a continuous sensation of obstruction and pain. By the aid of catechisms, Cross-mans, and burdensome observances, I was grooved laboriously into a secure and per-manent orthodoxy. My mental and spiritual parts were furrowed; but, alas! my physical part remained fallow. My growth in stature was left carelessly to my Maker, and pro-ceeded without a hint of artificial tribula-tion. This flaw in our educational system it is my ambition to remove. I have in-vented a mechanical adjustment of powerful magnetic needles, whose permanent appli-cation to the frame will render child, boy, ' or youth continuously sensible of physical growth. The feeling will be as though five minutes of acute toothache were diffused

over a space of months. A youth will literally develop into manhood through pins
and needles. We shall then have realized
the perfect organism of the Roman poet's
fancy, the —

Mens TORTA *in corpore* TORTO.

XVIII.

DEAD LANGUAGES.

A DEAD language: what a sad and solemn expression! Trite enough, I own; but to a reflective mind, none the less sad and solemn; for in the death of which it speaks are involved deaths untold, innumerable.

I can understand what is meant by "a Dead Sea;" and should suppose it to be a sheet of water cut off from all intercourse with the main ocean; never rising with its flow; never sinking with its ebb; never skimmed by the sail of commerce; never flapped by wing of wandering bird; undisturbed by the bustle of the restless world; but slumbering in a desolate wilderness, far from the track of caravan, or railway, or steamship, in a stagnant, and tide-forgotten and unheeded repose.

The chance-directed efforts of an enterprising traveller exhumed, but recently, the sculptured monuments of a dead civilization. We thus learned that Nineveh and Babylon were not only the homes of conquering kings, but the seats of tranquil learning and treasured science, before ever a fleet had sailed from Aulis, or the eagles had promised empire to the watcher on the green Palatine.

The language of priestly and kingly Etruria is revealed to us only by dim marks upon vase or tablet, or by melancholy inscriptions on sepulchral stones. That is, indeed, a language unquestionably dead.

But can such a term be applied to that Hellenic speech that in the Iliad has rolled, like the great Father of Waters, its course unhindered down three thousand years; that in Pindar still soars heavenwards, staring at the sun; that rises and falls in Plato with the long, sequacious music of an Æolian lute; that moves, stately and black-stoled, in Æschylus; that reverberates with laughter half-Olympian in Aristophanes; that pierces with a trumpet-sound in Demosthenes; that smells of crocuses in

Theocritus; that chirrups, like a balm-cricket, in Anacreon? If it be dead, then what language is alive?

Or again, is that old Italian speech dead and gone, that murmurs in Lucretius a ceaseless, solemn monotone of sea-shell sound; that in Virgil flows, like the Eridanus, calmly but majestically through rich lowlands, fringed with tall poplars and rimmed with grassy banks; that quivers to wild strings of passion in Catullus; that wimples like a beck in Ovid; that coos in Tibullus like the turtle; that sparkles in Horace like a well-cut diamond?

No: Heaven forbid it! No! Pile upon these twin daughters of Omphæan Zeus mountains of Grammars and Grammatical Exercises and Latin Readers and Greek Delectuses and Graduses and Dictionaries and Lexicons, until Ossa is dwarfed and Pelion is a wart. Let dull, colossal Pedantry — unconscious handmaid of the Abstract Bagman — with her tons of lumbal lead press heavily on the prostrate forms. For a while they may lie, breathless and exhausted; but when that is grown again wherein their great strength lay, then will they make a mighty effort, and fling high in air the accumulated scoria of ages: like a hailstorm in the surrounding sea will fall the fragments of a million gerund-stones; and the divine Twain will clothe themselves anew in their old strength and beauty, and sit down by the side of Zeus Omphæus, exulting in glory.

No, No! The music of Homer will die with the choral chants of the Messiah, and the strains of Pindar with the symphonies of Beethoven; *una dies dabit exitio* Aristophanes and Cervantes and Molière; the Mantuan will go hand in hand to oblivion with the Florentine, *divinus Magister cum Discipulo diviniore;* the Metamorphoses of Ovid will decay with the fantastic tale of Ariosto and the music of Don Giovanni; Horace will fade out of ken, linked arm in arm with that sweet fellow-epicure, Montaigne; Antigone will be forgotten maybe a short century before Cordelia; and Plato and Aristotle will be entombed beneath the Mausoleum that covers for ever the thoughts of Bacon, Kepler, Newton, and Laplace.

Moreover, before the last echoes of Greece and Rome shall have died away, a Slavonian horde will throng the Morea and the Cyclades; and in some crumbling cathedral, Catholicism will have chanted, for the last time, its own *Nunc dimittis*, in the grand imperial language of the City of the Seven Hills. .

When all this shall have come about, then may it be said with truth: " Rome is dead; and Athens is no more! the words of whose wise ones went out into all lands, and the songs of whose singing-men to the ends of the world: their pomp and their glory have gone down with them into the pit."

But, gentle Reader, long, long before this desolation shall have come about, you and I will be lying in a very sorry plight, with a strange and not beautiful expression on our human countenances: our quips, our cranks, our oddities all gone: quite chapfallen Yes, Friend, a very long while, indeed, before all this shall have come about.

XIX.

A VISION.

I WAS engaged one afternoon with my class in the study of that portion of the Æneid where the hero of the poem and the Sybil journey together by dim, uncertain moonlight, through the shadowy spaces of the under-world. And when the lesson was over, I begged of my boys to learn one splendid passage by heart; and leaning back my chair against the wall by the monotonous murmuring of their voices I was lulled into a strange reverie.

For in the darkness of the under-world I saw three figures moving slowly; and the one was gentle and benign of aspect, and in him I recognized the Divine Master of Mantua, " the honor and the light of poetry; " and the second was of a sad and stern countenance, who regarded the Master with

the admiration of a disciple; and the third
was like the Spirit of Myself.

And we had reached the rim of the
seventh circle; but from the inner circle
there rose a stench so terrible and noisome,
that I looked aside, if perchance there might
be a place of refuge. And in the dark wall
of stone there was a wide fissure like a
natural doorway; and over the fissure was
an inscription that I read with difficulty:
— PÆDAGOGORUM DEFUNCTORUM SEDES.
And the Divine Master went therein; and
the stern and sad Disciple followed; and I
went, holding by the garment of the latter.
And the fissure opened into a great vaulted
cavern, the farther end of which was
wrapped in gloom; and there were millions
of gigantic engines shaped like mill-stones,
and fitted each one with a handle; and the
handle of each was like the sail-arm of a
ship of war. And suspended from these
handles were the forms of men; and the
mill-stones were motionless, and the place
was empty of all sound. And suddenly,
from the farther gloom came rushing three
Erinnyes; and the one was armed with a

scourge, and the second with a yellow reed, and the other with what seemed to me a long thin broom, from which the handle had been shorn. And rushing to and fro, they scourged the suspended figures, and the place was suddenly filled with the whirring and the creaking of a million stone wheels. And the Disciple and I looked inquiringly in the face of the Master; but there was a look of unwonted pain in his benign countenance; and while we gazed wonderingly, he gave a shrill cry, and fell to the ground as one suddenly bereft of life.

And when at length his spirit revived, we lifted him gently, and guided him, in our turn, back through the fissure to the rim of the seventh circle. But we feared to ask him aught; seeing he had been sore troubled. But he, interpreting our secret thoughts, said in tones gentle and very sad: " They whom ye saw were PÆDAGOGI in the upper world; and their business it was to turn rapidly the gerund-stone. And forasmuch as I was born upon the skirts of Ignorance, and knew not the darkness of my day, therefore am I doomed to suffer sorely in the spirit with the turning of their gerund-stones. And I shall be PARSED thereby for twice a thousand years. And thereupon, the Pedant shall sit upon the Bagman, crushing him; and the Pedant shall choke in his own fat. And after that my spirit shall have rest.

At this moment I was roused by the sudden cessation of the wonted murmuring; and looking up, I saw the hour was on the stroke of one, and dismissed my boys to play.

XX.

THE SCHOOLMASTER'S LOVE-LETTER.

O mea cara, pulcra Mary,
Quàm vellem tecum concordare!
What bliss with thee, my Noun, to live,
Agreeing like the Adjective :
Not — Heaven forbid it ! — *genere,*
Si esset id possibile ;
But being one, and only so,
Concordaremus numero ;
And I'd agree with thee, my pet,
Casu ; ay, *casu quolibet :*
Likewise, as Relative, I'd fain
A Concord Personal maintain ;
Thus borrowing from two parts of speech
The partial harmony of each :
Maybe, from *qui* if more we'd borrow,
I'd be in *quod,* and thou in sorrow ;
For, Mary, better 'tis to give,
Than borrow with your relative.

Three grades are in Comparison;
My love admits of only one;
Only Superlative to me
Thy beauty is, like *optimè.*
O Mary, Mary, seal my fate;
Be candid, ere it be too late:
Is thy heart open to my suit,
✓ Free as an Ablative-Absolute?
Do, while I'm in the mood Optative,
Follow me, darling, in the dative:
Though I should be, for that condition,
Compounded with a Preposition:
Well, sure, of all the girls I see,
To each and all *præpono te,*
Te omnibus præpono, quarè
Thou art my Preposition, Mary.
Ah! dear, should everything go well,
And love should ring our marriage-bell,
Our happiness — to be prospective —
Would still, like *Ambo,* be defective:
But Plural-*caret* should we miss,
While Singular and complete in bliss?
No, no: for a while, my Pearl, my Jewel,
We'd linger patiently in the Dual;
Or ere a year had circled round,
  In cursu rerum naturali,

LOVE-LETTER. 253

Some morn or eve we should be found
  Happy, *in numero plurali.*
Then one in heart and soul and mind,
We'd grow in love as years Declined:
Moods of Command and Dubitation
We'd blot from out life's Conjugation:
Our love, like all things sweet and good,
Were best express'd, when Understood;
Timidly-noiseless, purely shy,
  Unheard of all, yet plain to see—
Like peeping Moon in fleecy sky,
  Or *II* in *Hora* and *Homine.*
But life, alas! to all that live,
Unlike true love, is Transitive:
To love, Intransitive love, is given
To Govern all in earth and heaven:
Yes, Mary; the ring, that would bind you to
      me,
  Were a poor Conjunction that death
      might sever —
A thin frail *et*, and a life-long *que;*
  But the link of our love would bind for
      ever.
And so, when came the certain *Finis,*
  We'd be content, my own, my dearie,

Sub uno tumulo duplex cinis,
  Two Supines, in one grave, *jacere.*
With folded hands upon heaveless breast,
  Side by side in our little earth bed,
Silent, as Gerunds in *Dum,* we'd rest,
  While the thunder of noisy years roll'd
    overhead:
And we'd sleep a sleep, still, calm, and sweet,
Till our graves grew forgotten and Obsolete;
Waiting the Voice that, as good men trust,
Shall make Active of Passive, and Spirit of
    dust.

XXI.

SUUM CUIQUE.

Nascitur, non fit, may be said as truly of the schoolmaster as of the poet. The popular, but mistaken idea is, that any young man, who at the age of twenty-one is well enough educated for a learned profession, but lacks the means or spirit to push his way in the world of Law or Medicine, may subside into a teacher of the Classics. Many young Englishmen think so themselves, and take clerical orders at the time of entering the despised profession, that they may escape from it, if on any white day a vicarage should fall from the clouds. These are they that are not born schoolmasters, but made schoolmasters of men.

In the matter of education, Scotland is, in many points, in advance of her southern neighbor. The middle-class preparatory schools of Dunedin are unapproachably superior to anything of the kind — if there be anything of the kind—in England. The teaching of the elementary classes in our High School and Schola Nova is even at present far superior to that of similar classes in any public schools in England with which I have been directly or indirectly acquainted ; and that includes almost all the public schools of importance in the country. With a few, but, I must own, very important modifications, our training of junior classes might be made almost perfect of its kind.

In our High School is still retained much of the beautiful vowel-music of Italian-Latin. The Greek Professor of our Dunedin University—faithful among the faithless, in *this* respect — can read a simile of Homer, without marring rhythm or ignoring accent.

In Scotland, also, the profession of teaching, though not sufficiently honored from a social point of view, is rightly considered as *specific*, and calling for *specific qualifications*, When Adam and Carson of our High School, Melvin of Aberdeen, and Carmichael of

our own Schola Nova, first apprenticed
themselves to their craft, they left no plank
behind them for recrossing at a favorable
opportunity to ease or affluence in an extraneous calling. They put their hands to
the plough, these simple men; and there
was no looking back. They devoted themselves to the business of classical instruction as single-heartedly as did the Apostles
to the dissemination of Christian doctrine.
They knew well enough that spiritual darkness abounded, but they left its enlighten-
ment to another calling—the only one that
in the dignity of usefulness takes precedence
of their own.

And one of them lived too short a life;
but they all lived lives laborious and useful
and honorable. From dawn to sunset of
their day of toil they sowed the seed, or
drave the plough, or brake with harrows
the obstructive glebe. And when at length
it *was growing dark*, these husbandmen dismissed their little reapers and gleaners;
and gat them home, wearied; and turned
to; and fell on sleep. No foretaste of
earthly glory sweetened the bitterness of

the last cup. From modest homes they were borne, unnoticed, to modest graves. But the statues of these Cincinnatus-teachers stand, not unwreathed with laurel, in the Valhalla of great and good and single-hearted school-masters. With all the other good men and true. And the Valhalla is not in Dunedin, Reader; but in a great and distant city; a city not built with hands; a city more beautiful by far than beautiful Dunedin.

About a furlong from my own lodgings, in a room as near to heaven, burns the midnight lamp of one who could read a play of Sophocles ere I could inarticulately scream. He has read more of ancient lit-erature than many literary men have read of English. He has purified his Greek seven times in the fire. He has resuscitated many Aorists, that for centuries had lain dormant under mossy stones. He has passed, alone and fearless, through waste places, where no footfall had echoed for a hundred years. In England, nothing but a special interpo-sition of Providence could have saved this scholar from the Bench of Bishops: in Scot-land, nothing short of personal violence could have pushed him into a Professorial Chair. The fact is, this man, with all his learning, is bowed down with the weight of a most unnational modesty. Indeed, of this quality, as of erudition, there is as much contained in his well as would serve to irrigate his native country. Heaven knows what he might have been, had he consented in earlier life to play in public the cymbals of claptrap and the tom-tom of self-conceit. But his voice was never heard in the Palaverium of Dunedin. My friend, in fact, was ostracized by his fellow-citizens of the Modern Athens. You may hear of him at Jena, Göttingen, or Heidelberg; but, in perusing the list of Doctors of our own Universities, after running your finger down some columns of mediocre Rabbis, you will experience a sensation of relief in missing the name of Veitch. *Præfulget ibi nomen eo ipso, quòd non cernitur.*

In day-schools, like the two great institutions of Dunedin, where the boys only give a morning and noon attendance for five days in the week, there is no call for the clerical element whatsoever. Their pupils combine the advantages of a public school with the inestimable and civilizing influences of home life. As their parents and guardians may reasonably be supposed to be in all cases Christian, there would seem to be no need for religious instruction in their school-hours; and it might be thought sufficient, if such Institutions opened the work of each day with the reverent reading of some chapter of the New Testament, and a short and appropriate prayer; and if a weekly lesson were given from the historical portions of the older Scriptures. Not to speak of the heterogeneous admixture of doctrinal lessons with those in Latin syntax and Rule of Three, the boys are supposed to hear family prayers each morning and evening; to attend Divine Service regularly; and to hear the Bible read and expounded by a devout father or mother. The hearing of one parable from the gentle voice of the latter is worth all the religious instruction that a master can impart in class, where in the hearts of boys the spirit of gentleness is too apt to succumb to the sterner spirit of class-ambition.

However, the question is different in regard to large schools where children are, with questionable propriety, removed entirely from home. Here I can perfectly understand how well the moral and religious training of pupils might be entrusted to discreet clerical hands; and would allow to the chaplain of such an Institution *a pre-eminence in rank and emolument,* as due to the sacredness of his calling. There would be some studies, also, in which he could give valuable help; as, in that of Biblical and even Secular history; and over all he might exert a wholesome influence. But I am wholly at a loss to account for the fact, that in England, the teaching of the classical languages should be considered as almost necessarily devolving upon the clergy. Why should it require Holy Orders to fit a man to teach the heathen tongues of Athens and Rome, any more than to teach the Christian tongues of France, Germany or Italy? or, indeed, any more than to teach drawing or music or dancing? Greek and Latin are important elements in the education of a gentleman, but they enter very indirectly into the training of a Christian. They may

lead a man part of the way to the Wool-
sack; but they cannot carry him one step
on the road that leads to the Everlasting
Gates. No: many children have gone in
thereat, that never stumbled through a declension; or that stumbled through one,
and nothing more: many men, that in boyhood fell through the Asses' Bridge, have,
in spite of corpulence, passed safely over
the suspended camel's hair, that breaks only
beneath iniquity: many dear, illiterate old
saints have outstripped wits and critics and
scholars and theologians on their journey to
an unaspirated Heaven.

But it may be contended, that in a Christian country it is requisite to Christianize the whole curriculum of education.
Granted: I question, however, from my own
experience, whether the means taken are
suited to the ends, and whether we may not
so Christianize our education as to secular-
ize our Christianity. I have known of a
Clerical Master who, on a Sunday afternoon, could set a little congregation weeping with the rich mellowness of his voice
and the depth of his pathos; and many

members of his little congregation had wept
during the previous week, and would weep
during the following week, beneath the
force of his arm. Should the same fountain bring forth sweet and bitter?

One of my Classical Masters at St. Edward's was ordinarily mild and gentle; but
he was abnormally severe on the days when
we said our *Crossman,* as the Catechism
was appropriately named. There was less
danger to us in a false concord or a false
quantity, than in unwitting heterodoxy in
the matter of the Sacraments. This was
not a method calculated to render religious
instruction pleasing in our eyes: and, indeed, it was very far from pleasing: it was
associated with ideas of fear, and curiously
jumbled with associations of Sallust and
Xenophon. It was of the earth, earthy.

But, apart from the interests of children,
what can the effect be upon clerical schoolmasters of their having to devote nearly
their whole time and energies to the inculcation of secular studies? Does it never
strike them that there is an incongruity
between the solemn obligations they once

took, and the secular occupations they now follow? I can hardly think that St. Paul, if he were permitted to abide with us awhile, would lay hands upon any young Timothy, and enjoin him strictly to edify the brethren in turning Gibbon into Tacitean prose, or Shakespeare into Greek Iambics.

Again; when a distinguished Fellow of some great Oxford or Cambridge college condescends to accept a Head-Mastership, he does so on the tacit understanding that he will in due time be rewarded with clerical promotion. Maybe over a space of some twelve years, his capacities as · a teacher will be honorably attested by the Class Lists of the Universities, and a sprinkling of Camdens, Porsons, Hertfords, and Irelands: he will have successfully conducted a very lucrative establishment of Boarders; he will have thrown a flood of Latin light upon some ill-appreciated *équivoques grossières* in the Thesmophoriazusæ: he will have plastered some severe masterpiece of Æschylus with annotatory stucco; he will have published a most interesting and popular series of Lectures on *The Rite of Con-*

firmation, or the Laying on of Hands — and
I may as well warn the reader, that the latter part of this title is to be understood in
an episcopal rather than a pædagogic sense.
When he has thus reached his zenith of
fame and usefulness in one calling, he is
translated to another, entailing duties and
requiring talents of an entirely different
kind. How many a Head-Master, beloved
of his senior pupils, has passed the autumn
of his days in worrying the clergy of a
grumbling diocese?

At all events, if such translations be right
in themselves, why should they be confined
in their operation? We might transfer a veteran Barrister to the Presidency of the Royal
Academy; or reward a decayed Admiral
with the Chancellorship of the Exchequer.

There is another light in which to view
the subject. There are a few instances, a
very few, in our great English schools,
where men of good repute in scholarship
refrain from taking Holy Orders. They
might take these orders any day it pleased
their bishop to hold an ordination. They
would rarely or never be called upon to do

clerical duty. Then why on earth are they
so stupid as not to take a step which would
at once improve their social standing, and
open for them a path to distinction? Why,
the ridiculous fellows carry an old-fashioned
conscience trailing awkwardly at their sides;
and, of course, it gets between their legs,
and trips them up; and it serves the stupid
fellows right.

A simpleton might argue, that, by such
a course of proceeding, they devote themselves entirely to the business of teaching,
and demonstrate a special call to that special
occupation. But this argument is obviously
ludicrous. For, were it correct, we should
see the highest prizes in the scholastic walk
opened to these self-denying laymen. But
these latter are the very men to whom, by
a discerning public, those high prizes are
closed and barred. For there is some mystic *Open Sesame*, that unbars the gates to
all Head-Masterships; and the words are
known only to the clergy; who, *with the
consent of the Laity*, guard their secret, and
pass it on and round, in whispers, only to
one another.

Not many years ago, the patrons of a large proprietary school in the West of England offered their head-mastership to a very distinguished scholar, a friend of my own, on condition that he would take Holy Orders. It was more than insinuated that these Orders would merely affect the fashion of his neck-tie, and the prejudices of an enlightened public. My friend was a man of middle age, with habits and character thoroughly formed, and with as much idea of turning clergyman as of buying the practice of a dentist. Consequently, the offer, though pecuniarily a very tempting one, was not accepted. My friend is prosecuting his journey heavenwards with a well-stored brain; a rather ill-stored scrip; a white conscience; and a black tie. For my own part, I regard such martyrdom as utterly out of place in a practical age. When the head-mastership is next vacant, I trust the patrons will make a similar offer to me. They have merely to name their salary — and their Bishop.

XXII.

THE SOCIAL POSITION OF SCHOOLMASTERS.

MANY of my School Vacations I passed
in Bruges and Brussels, and made the acquaintance from time to time of boys of
my own age attending the *Athénées* or
Public Schools of these towns. Indeed, my
own brother received at such schools the
greater part of his education. The Masters
were laymen; in a country next to Spain
perhaps the most bigotedly Catholic in
Europe. The means of coercion at their
disposal seemed to my young English ideas
barbarously simple. No birch; no cane;
not even the ridiculously mild strap. How
on earth could pupils learn Latin Versification, or any other useful accomplishment,
without such obviously requisite stimu-
lants? However, their Classes of Rhetoric,
or Senior Classes, *did* turn out well-edu-

cated and most gentlemanly-mannered men.
But the strangest thing to me was that the
masters were never spoken of as occupying
any peculiar or comical position in society.
It. never seemed to strike a boy to speak
in terms of ridicule of his schoolmaster any
more than of his Clergyman or Medical
Attendant. In fact, society at large seemed
unconsciously to regard the Master of an
Athénée as *an ordinary gentleman*, neither
more nor less.

One of the most polished and accomplished men I have ever had the honor of
knowing was my brother's Music-master,
whose lessons were given at a rate that
would appear to us ludicrously small. He
associated on terms of perfect intimacy with
families of very ancient lineage in the neighborhood of Bruges. He used to describe in
the most humorous fashion the treatment
he occasionally met with in English *salons*,
whose occupants, of undoubtedly high position at home, were temporarily residing
abroad for reasons of financial retrenchment.

I have had many relatives educated entirely in Florence, and have heard that the

masters, who visited the leading schools there, held a social position in that not unaristocratic city quite equal to that of an ordinary barrister amongst ourselves. And these masters had no ecclesiastical title to raise them in the social scale.

In England, at a very early period, the birch and cane were engrafted upon our educational system. They naturally made the position of a schoolmaster odious in the sight of children, and somewhat ludicrous in the eyes of the world, and especially so in the eyes of women. Now the English character is essentially practical, but by no means bigoted to logic. Their political Constitution might be theoretically assailed on many points; but it works satisfactorily as a whole. Their Church is an obvious compromise: its Articles are allowedly incongruous: but it works well. It certainly never produces a Xavier or a Carlo Borromeo: no saint with apostolic halo round his brow: but it also lacks the superlative vices that Rome cherishes in her catholic bosom. In the matter of education, England shows an equal disregard of logic and an equal determination of working good ends by any practical means. The position of a schoolmaster needed backing up, it seemed, in some way. Then make the schoolmaster a Clergyman. Never mind the absurdity of calling upon a man to swear that he will spend and be spent in preaching the Glad Tidings, when *he* knows, and everybody knows, that he will pass his life in teaching the Rudiments of Greek and Latin. With a practical people such obligations are generally understood in a practical way; and the practical way of understanding them seems, in this one instance, to lie in ignoring them partially or altogether.

There can be little doubt that, without the aid of clerical prestige, no body of men could have continued to command public respect in spite of the odium and ridicule attached to such flagrantly cruel implements as the cane and birch. The former of these, as I know to my cost, is painful in the extreme; and the infliction of the latter is always brutal, and **very** often abominably indecent.

Now, in Scotland, whatever our faults may be — and *Scottish* writers on the London press purge us from time to time of our conceit — we are acknowledged to be a logical race. Consequently, we call a schoolmaster a schoolmaster. We no more think of allowing him to take fictitious orders, than we should think of giving a haberdasher the fictitious title of M.D.: and yet a schoolmaster in Scotland has certainly need of any aid that could be rendered for the improvement of his social status. The latter is far below that of any other professional body. Yet, low as is comparatively the social position of the Scottish schoolmaster, he can point to his ridiculous but almost innocuous leather strap, and boast that he has contrived therewith to maintain discipline and stimulate to exertion, while a wealthier body, with rich endowments and ecclesiastical prestige, have made unsparing use of two instruments, whose barbarity as far exceeds that of his own strap, as the income of an Eton Provost exceeds that of a Rector of our High School.

But to revert to the consideration of

the social rank of a master in a Scottish grammar-school. The Rectors of the two chief Edinburgh Schools are exceptions to the ordinary rule. They enjoy a social rank befitting the dignity of their official duties. But how is it that the masters of classics, mathematics, and modern languages, in these and similar institutions, take by general consent a lower place at feasts than a medical man of little practice, and an advocate of few briefs?

In the social estimate of a whole order of men, I am inclined to think the world at large cannot be *altogether* wrong. There is generally fault on both sides. If then we schoolmasters *are* at fault, it would be of use if we could only hit upon our weak point. We might then give it a fair and serious consideration; and use means, if they could be suggested, for remedying the evil.

I have heard it said by a gentleman of very high position, and of reputed scholarship, that the subordinate master in a great Scottish school is only expected by a Scottish public to be a man of ordinary attainments, who can drill his pupils well in the rudiments, and just keep pace with them in their higher reading. While such melancholy opinions are generally entertained of our craft, it is especially incumbent upon us to endeavor by our teaching and our lives to belie them. It is because we too often give in, for want of courage or proper pride, to such a condemnation of our order that we continue to be members of a Pariah profession. We are too often contented with the limited intellectual stores that were laid in at College. We too often go uninquiringly through a dull routine ; caring little whether or no we carry the inclinations and sympathies of our boys along with us, so long as we get through the prescribed work, and preserve a mechanical discipline. We are not impressed with the fact, that a schoolmaster cannot be too learned, too accomplished. Under any circumstances, something of the tedious must creep into the routine of school-work, and it will need a wide field of continual reading to enable one to illustrate and vivify daily lessons, that vary from the declension of *penna* to the study of the Agamemnon.

The pupils at our chief public schools study German and French. Should a master of the two great ancient languages be ignorant of linguistic studies, in which his pupils may be proficient? No: he should outstrip them immeasurably in every department of study that bears upon his own. He should be so impressed with the dignity of his calling,—and what calling, save the cure of souls is more dignified?—so full of chastened respect for himself, as to command the respect of his pupils, though he may fail for a while to command that of the more unthinking of the public. If we could only work ourselves up to some such standard, we might then gradually dispense with that little leathern instrument, that still keeps a burr of ridicule attached to our black gowns.

But, stop: am I again travelling to Utopia? Let me turn my hobby's head, and gallop back to dear Dunedin. When a man's liver is out of order, what on earth is the use of his doctor's telling him to keep early hours; to use a cold tub; to live temperately, and take frequent out-door exercise? Why, his grandmother might have suggested that. What the man wants is a blue pill or two. They can be taken in a minute; and he need not materially change his dietetics. Could not some such violent but easy remedy be suggested for the cure of our social abasement? Certainly. Why should Baring-out be confined to boys? or Strikes to Artisans? A fig for political economy! Let us form ourselves into a League and proclaim a general STRIKE OF SCHOOLMASTERS! There will be some sneaking recusants among us: but we will brain them with their own dictionaries.

Some Summer morning Scotland will awake, and find every grammatical fountain frozen. What fun it will be for the boys! For a week the parents may outface the inconvenience; but in a month the animal, always latent in boyhood, will be growing rampant and outrageous. Gradually will it develop, unsoothed by the influences of grammar, unchecked by the sterner influences of our magic leather. No father will be safe in his own house. The smaller boys will be smoking brown paper in the drawing-room, and the older boys wallowing in Bass and cavendish in the lower kitchen.

Meanwhile, calmly reposing in the stillness of his back parlor, M'Gillicuddy will be putting the finishing stroke to that folio edition of Cornelius Nepos, on which his fame in after ages is to rest; and I, in my aërial lodgings, shall be setting to Greek iambics the moral aphorisms of the great Tupper, whose terseness and originality are the wonder of a grateful people.

Our hospitable Provost, like his predecessor in olden days when the English were marching north, will hold a meeting of troubled citizens. They will meet in arms: each father will be provided with his life-preserver of cut leather. One speaker will tell how nouns are at a fabulous premium; that an adjective may not be had for love or money. Another will tell the horrible tale, how whole families have for weeks subsisted on the smallest prepositions. They will attempt a compromise. We shall decline treating on such terms. They will surrender unconditionally; and our terms

—monstrous as they may seem — shall be as follows : —

A Schoolmaster, who shall have graduated at an University, shall hereafter be addressed, personally or epistolarily, with the courtesy usually shown to a second-rate Solicitor or a briefless Advocate.

Whosoever shall wittingly and wilfully offend against the above decree, let him for the first offence be dismissed after due admonition ; but, on a second offence being proven, let him be sentenced to parse verbatim the folio edition of M'Gillicuddy's Nepos, declining all nouns, conjugating all verbs, and repeating all syntax rules, *usque ad Rei ipsius et totius Curiæ nauseam.*

XXIII.

TINT, TINT, TINT.

It is now twelve years ago that I was for the first time brought face to face with a class some fifty in number, of little Latin novices. They all regarded me with sensations of wonderment and awe: they had but a faint idea, luckily, of the terror with which I regarded them. I had, certainly, the recollections of my own long elementary training to guide me in my proceedings; and I had the traditions of the school, to which I had been recently appointed as master, to direct my uncertain steps. But the recollections of my own training were all tinged with melancholy; and with the traditions of my new sphere of duty I was but imperfectly acquainted.

In the middle of my class-room stood a machine, somewhat resembling a patent en gine for the simultaneous polishing of many knives; and I was desired to take a firm grasp of its wooden handle, and to turn it with vigor and rapidity. And an implement of simple leather was put into my hands, by the dexterous application of which I was to quicken the apprehensions of such children as might be uninfluenced by the monotonous music of my gerund-stone.

And for many a day, obedient to tradition and to my orders, I turned rapidly the wooden handle, and flourished vigorously the simple implement to the very best of my ability. But, strange to say, although I was then youthful and strong, and eaten up with a superfluous zeal for my calling, I could never turn the machine without its creaking painfully; and whenever I applied my leathern implement to a child's palm, I was immediately conscious of a thrill, as of electricity, that ran from my finger-tips to the very centre of my nervous system; and sometimes, after the performance of such an ordinary act of duty, I would find myself standing before my pupils with a heightened color upon my face, and a tingling in my ears; and to a looker-on I should have appeared as one ashamed of having done some questionable deed.

Finding all my efforts unavailing to work smoothly and noiselessly my mechanical engine of instruction, I at length relinquished it altogether; and it has been now standing for years in a side-room adjoining my place of business, and is covered over with cobwebs, and rusted at the juncture of the stone and handle.

To supply the place of its simple mechanism, I brought to bear upon my pupils all the moral and intellectual means at my disposal. I spared myself neither in the matter of time nor trouble in my endeavors to educe the dormant faculties of my charges; and enjoying as I did for many years a bodily health impervious to fatigue, and having a keen sympathy with boyhood, I succeeded more and more until I almost ceased at length to regret the disappearance of my gerund-stone.

But the more I gave satisfaction to myself, the less I gave satisfaction to the majority of my so-called patrons; the guard-

ians of my young pupils. From time to
time, when I was indulging in a dream of
appreciated toil, I heard of complaints being circulated by such as were favorers of
mechanism in instruction. Pupils, in whose
progress I had begun to take a keen interest, were from time to time removed without a word of explanation or the civility of
a farewell. " They were not *grounded*,"
said these waggish but unmannerly guardians; meaning all the while, " They were
not *ground*."

I had almost begun to despair of my
system, and to think that I had mistaken
my calling; and was casting about my eyes
for some honest trade to which I might
apprentice myself, when one afternoon my
class was honored with a lengthened visit
from a gentleman of acknowledged rank and
worth and judgment. After the lesson was
over, I complained to this distinguished
visitor that my system of conveying instruction, as being natural and philosophic,
was popularly considered a more difficult
one for a pupil than the ancient turning of
a piece of mechanism. My visitor, who had

a son under my charge, stated his firm conviction that my system was not only likely
to produce better results, but was also in its
operation far more easy and interesting for a
young pupil to follow. For that moment I
felt re-assured, and determined never again
to regret the absence of my gerund-stone.

And now to treat of the loss of my other
auxiliary implement. The application of
this latter, I can honestly say, was never
made excepting with the view of stimulating
ever-dormant energies, and of repressing
tendencies to chronic negligence or miscon-
duct. I considered myself as an abstraction;
as the embodied representative of the class;
and used the implement only to protect the
interests of the latter, which suffered, to my
mind, whenever one of its members, by
carelessness or lack of study, turned upon
himself that stream of time and energy that
should have run uninterruptedly to the
irrigation of the body corporate. In fact,
I made myself the dividend in a long division sum, whose divisor was *duty;* the quo-
tient, I found, was *teacher* + *superintendent,*
and the remainder, *personal identity,* which

was very small in comparison with the divisor, and might practically be ignored. So, when a little fellow walked after me for a few days at the striking of the bell, with his hands beneath imaginary coat-tails in imitation of my gait, I considered him as only joking with me in my capacity of *remainder;* and I merely asked him to desist, as otherwise I should make fun of him in revenge; and he desisted. And when a boy wrote my name upon the desk, I was contented with showing him how he had mis-spelt it; and he rubbed it out at my request. And when a boy, years ago, put his tongue into his cheek after an admonition, I showed his comrades what little control he had over that organ; knowing as I did that he intended to protrude it on the side that would have been invisible to me. And I may state that such trifling incidents were of so rare occurrence, that I could enumerate them all upon the fingers of one hand.

But still, although I was conscious that I used the implement with good intent, and aware that it was similarly used by men who were my superiors in age, and certainly not my inferiors in kindliness and sympathy with boyhood, I was haunted with an idea that the use of it was founded on an error in our system of instruction; and I was long pondering where the error could lie; and I found the subject far more difficult than I had at first supposed; and I confess it still to be a problem difficult of solution.

I was in this frame of mind one day, when, according to an unalterable rule, there came under the influence of the electric implement a little, quiet, well-behaved, and intelligent foreigner. The application had scarce been made, when a young comrade — bless the lad! — gave vent to an unmistakeable hiss! Order, of course, was immediately and energetically re-established. But in my walk that afternoon by the sea, and in many a lonely walk afterwards, I thought about that little foreigner and his courageous comrade. And I thought how that little foreigner, returning to his own land, the ancient home of courtesy and gentle manners, would tell his friends of our rude, northern ways. And I tremble at the idea of my usage of the Electric Leather being narrated in the hearing of one of those terrible Colonels, whom their Emperor holds with difficulty on the leash. For I thought if ever our great metropolis were in their hands, how ill it would fare with all therein that turned the gerund-stone, and with those therein that bare my hapless surname. And the name of these is Legion. And knowing that the comrade was no vulgar and low-natured boy, I felt sure in my heart that there was at least something right in the impulse that had pushed him into danger and disobedience. But still I was afraid of allowing sentimentalism or impulsiveness on my part to take the place of duty however stern and unpalatable.

I was standing not alone one morning in the lobby of my own home, just before leaving for the day's work. A great-coat of mine was hanging from the wall. My Companion, in a playful mood, put a small, white hand into one of its pockets, and drew a something out; then thrust it back hurriedly as though it had been a something venomous. And over a very gentle face passed a look of surprise not unmingled with reproof; but the reproof gave way almost momently to the wonted smile. But I long remembered the mild reproof upon that gentle face; for it was an expression very seldom seen there; and it came afterwards to be numbered with other sad and sweet memories.

Meanwhile, at the end of the last bench upon my class sat a boy who was very backward in his learning. He was continually absent upon what seemed to me frivolous pretences. These absences entailed upon me much additional trouble. I had occasionally to keep him and a little remnant in the room when the others had gone out to play; to make up to him and them for lost time. And on one occasion my look was very cross, and my speech very short; for it seemed to me provoking that children should be so backward in their Latin. And when the work was over, and we two were left alone, he followed me to my desk, and said: "You have no idea, sir, how weak I am." And I said: "Why, my boy, you look stout enough." But he answered: "I am really very weak, sir; far weaker than

I look !" and there was a pleading earnestness in his words that touched me to the heart; and, afterwards, there was an unseen chord of sympathy that bound the master to the pupil, who was still very dull at Latin.

And still he would be absent; at times, for a day or two together. But it excited no surprise. For the boy seemed to sit almost a stranger among his fellows; and in play-hours seemed to take no interest in boyish games. And by and by he had been absent for some weeks together. But I was afraid to ask concerning him; thinking he might have been removed, as many boys had been, without a letter of explanation, or his shaking me by the hand. And one morning I received a letter with a broad black edge, telling me that he had died the day previously of a virulent contagious fever.

So when school was over, I made my way to his whilome lodging; and stood at the door, pondering. For the fever, of which the child had died, had been to me a Death-in-life, and had passed like the Angel of old over my dwelling, but, unlike that angel, had spared my first-born, and only-born. And because the latter sat each evening on my knee, I was afraid of the fever, and intended only to leave my card, as a mark of respectful sympathy. But the good woman of the house said: "Nay, nay, Sir, but ye'll see the Laddie;" and I felt drawn by an influence of fatherhood more constraining than a father's fears, and followed the good woman into the small and dim chamber where my pupil was lying. And, as I passed the threshold, my masterhood slipt off me like a loose robe; and I stood very humble and pupil-like, in that awful Presence, that teacheth a wisdom to babes and sucklings, to which our treasured lore is but a jingling of vain words. And, when left alone, I drew near the cheerless and dismantled bed, on which my pupil lay asleep in his early coffin. And he looked very calm and happy, as though there had been to him no pain in passing from a world where he had had few companions and very little pleasure. And I knew that his boyhood had been as dreary as it had been short; and I thought that the good woman of his lodging had perhaps been his only sympathizing friend at hand. And I communed with myself whether aught I had done could have made his dulness more dull. And I felt thankful for the chord of sympathy that had united us, unseen, for a little while. But, in a strange and painful way, I stood rebuked before the calm and solemn and unrebuking face of the child on whom I had frowned for his being backward in his Latin.

That evening, as usual, my own child was seated on my knee, making sunrise out of sunset for myself and his Mother's mother. And the table was alive with moo-cows, and bow-wows, and silly sheep. And we sang snatches of impossible songs; or hid ourselves behind chairs and curtains in a barefaced and · undeceitful manner. And the Penates at my hearth, that were chipped and broken, blinked merrily by the firelight; and the child was taken to his tiny bed; and the chipped Penates, thereupon, slowly faded out of view, and disappeared among the cinders.

And I sat, musing; alone. And yet not all alone. For in the chair, where recently

had been sitting the mother of my child's
Mother, there sat a grey, transparent Shape.
And the Shape and I were familiar friends.
He had sat with me many a time from midnight until when the morning had come
peeping through the green lattice. And he
had peopled all the chambers of my house
with sad thoughts and black-stoled memories. So, never heeding my familiar friend,
I sat, staring in the fire, and thinking.

And I thought, sadly and almost vindic-
tively, of the dreary years of my own early
boyhood, with their rope of sand, and the
mill-wheel that had ground no corn. And
I remembered how at times there would
come to me in my exile the sound of my
brother's laugh, and the sweeter music of
my Mother's voice. But I remembered
thankfully, that through years of monotonous work and rough usage I had enjoyed
sound health, and had had companions, with
whom I had walked, and talked, and
romped, and fought, cheerily.

And I wondered whether I should be
spared to see my own child grow to be a

merry and frank-hearted little fellow; to
hear the music of his ringing laugh; to see
his face flushed with rude but healthful
sport; to hear of him as beloved for many
boyish virtues, and reproved, not unlov-
ingly, for his share of boyish faults. And I
longed to be climbing with him the hill of
Difficulty; and lightening the ascent for
him with varied converse; resting now and
then to look down upon the valley, or to
let him gather blue-bells that grew on the
hillside.

And then I thought of a boy, who had
sat of late on the last bench in my class-
room; with a timid and scared look beside
his bluff and bold companions; who had
stood in the noisy play-ground, lonely as
in a wilderness; whom I had seen that
afternoon in his early coffin, with the seal
upon his forehead of Everlasting Peace;
the peace that passeth all understanding.

So I determined; from the recollections
of my own dreary boyhood; for the mild
reproof that once had clouded momently
very gentle eyes; for the love I bare my

own little one; and for the calm and unrebuking face I had seen that afternoon; that
I would do as little as possible in the exercise of my stern duties to make of life a
weariness to young children; and especially
to such as should be backward in their
Latin.

XXIV.

THE PRESSURE OF GENTLENESS.

A CLOSE relation of my own was for twelve years an officer in almost the severest of all continental services. In that chivalric army is conserved a traditional discipline, whose details would appal a democrat, and the exactions of which could only be endured by an obedient and military race. He tells me that, in his long experience, he only met with one Captain, who in dealing with his company avowedly ignored all means of physical coercion. On this Captain's breast were the Orders of two kingdoms and two empires: after one well-fought day he had been voted by acclamation as a candidate for the Order of the Iron Crown, which he would have obtained had he added his own signature to those of all his brother officers; and yet so soft-hearted was this *Chevalier sans peur* that any slattern beggar-woman could draw from him an ill-spared florin. In a village, where a portion of the regiment were once quartered, the good Curé, at the close of a sermon on Christian Character, told his flock that, if they wished to see Christianity in action, they might see it in a Captain of Grenadiers, who clothed their poorest children with his pocket-money, and whose closest companion was ignorant of his good deeds. This Captain's company was noted as being the best-dressed and the best-conducted in the regiment. There were at Solferino (and there are, alas! such cases in all engagements) cases of gallant but stern officers that fell by a traitorous bullet from behind. There was not one man in the company of this Captain that would not have taken in his stead a bullet aimed at him from the front.

A year and a half ago I met in Yorkshire an invalid young sailor. From his smooth face, short statue, and attenuated form, I should have taken him for a senior midship-man. To my complete astonishment I found he was commander of a Pacific liner,

with a numerous crew under his orders, and
in receipt of a splendid income. He had
been third in command, when the two sen-
iors had taken fever, and his gallantry under
trying circumstances of all kinds had pro-
cured his unusually early promotion. I dis-
cussed with him the theory of discipline.
He considered physical chastisement as brutal; swearing as un-Christian; and hector-
ing as unmanly. "The man who cannot
control himself is not fit to command a
crew," he said, tritely and truly. I looked
in wonder at this shrimp of a man, that was
speaking with such calm confidence. "I
never," he continued, "raise my voice above
its usual tone to enforce an order." He was
worn to skin and bone by a chest disorder
of long continuance, which he considered
would close his life at no distant date. I
could have pushed him over with a rude
jostle of my elbow. But there was something in his face that told you unmistaka-
bly he was not the man with whom to take
a liberty. He gave me a remarkable anec-
dote of himself. His ship was alongside of
an American liner in the Liverpool docks.

The Yankee captain was dining with him, and the conversation fell upon the means of maintaining order in a crew. The Yankee scouted all means but the stick. He and his mates used on principle the most brutal means of coercion. During their argument, the steward came to announce that the English crew were fighting the Yankees on the neighboring vessel. The captains went on deck, and the Englishman, slinging himself by a rope, alighted in the midst of an uproarious crowd. " Well, my men," said he, " so you are making beasts of yourselves, and disgracing your captain." And the big fellows slunk off without a word to their own vessel, and one or two of the ringleaders were set for an hour or two to swab the decks. But of the quarreling tars there was not a man but could have lifted his wee captain, and dropped him overboard without an effort. I trust to God he may yet be living, and may long be spared, as a specimen of a quiet, resolute, English, Christian Skipper.

My chiefest friend at school was a man of widest mental culture, of even temper, and of sound judgment. Among his friends and my own at Trinity I knew a few men of a similarly high stamp. I remember one man in particular, in whom the Scholar and the Christian so curiously blended, that it would be difficult to say where his Latin ended and his religion began. He was a spiritual and mental Merman. But if I were called upon to name the Aristides of my life-acquaintance, I should name a man, whom I never knew till I had crossed the Tweed. I believe it would be as hard to warp a Carlyle into sentimental or religious cant, and a prophet-Cumming into common-sense and modesty, as to twist the nature of my friend into petty words or illiberal action.

He was once the superintendent of a public educational institution. He had been present one day in the drill-ground, where an honest sergeant with a good deal of superfluous bluster was putting a little regiment through its facings. When the boys were dismissed, the sergeant approached his superior, and said : " Excuse the liberty, Sir, but really, when you are more used to boys, you'll find that you must put more pepper into what you do and say." "Well," said my friend, "every man has his own way: for my own part, I don't believe in pepper."

A few weeks afterwards, the Principal was in his library, when the sergeant was ushered in. "I've come, Sir," said the latter, " to ask a favor. Those boys are a little troublesome at times. If you'd be kind enough just to stand at your drawing-room window for a few minutes when drill was going on, it would do a deal of good; if you'd only stand for a few minutes, reading a newspaper."

Ah! worthy sergeant; your pepper won't do after all. No, friend, keep it for your vegetables, and use it then in moderation.

I hold that men may be called of God to more offices than the holy one of the Christian ministry. There was an under-officer at my old school, who to me seemed always to partake largely of some of the finest attributes of the gentleman. He had failed through continued ill-health in business as a bookseller, and was a well-read man. He was uniformly civil and respectful to us,

senior scholars; but, while we could tip
and bribe others, we could never venture on
the liberty of an unadorned surname with
him.   This man was called to the humble
office of maintaining order in the school-
yard. So there are men called to command
men on the field of battle, and boys in the
school-room.   I have met with a schoolmaster in Scotland who could govern a
crowd of boys in one room, though they
might be divided into scattered groups, and
engaged in varied work; and his only implements of discipline were a word or two
of good-natured banter or kindly encour-
agement, and occasionally a calm and stern
rebuke.   I have been much struck by the
expression of his opinion, that physical coercion cannot be dispensed with altogether.
In defiance, however, of a kindness, a sagacity, and a judgment that I respect, I do
most firmly believe that the necessity for
physical chastisement rests mainly upon
two blemishes in our ordinary school system: the mechanical nature of our routine
of work; and the crowding of our class-
rooms.   In the latter respect we are more

at fault than our English brethren; in the former we are far less sinning. In the teaching of our elementary classes we employ far more spirit, and far less wood; and I wish I could add, *no leather.* There is less of a gulf between pupil and master. The severest means of physical chastisement at the disposal of the latter is almost innocuous. But mild as our implement may be from the point of view of physical pain inflicted, its employment is of necessity associated with some degree of odium, and a more formidable amount of ridicule. I am convinced that many children imagine that we, schoolmasters, were as naturally born with tawse, as foxes with tails. Did you ever see children in a nursery play at school? The rule seems to be for the elder brother to play our part; and that part is limited to the fun or business of flogging all his little sisters.

We have gone a great way already in Scotland in the way of civilized teaching, in forbearing to use an instrument of acute pain and an instrument of indecent brutality. Let us make a further advance, and if we can invent some intellectual and moral substitute for our ridiculous scourges, let us send the latter in bundles to the public schools of England, to be there adopted when their system is sufficiently ripened by a few extra centuries of Christianity. Let us close their scholastic nakedness with the last rags of our barbarism. Our boys will be none the less manly and respectful. Flogging can never instil courage into a child, but it has helped to transform many an one into a sneak. And sneakishness is a vice more hard to eradicate than obduracy. So far from curing an ill-conditioned boy of rude and vulgar ways, it is calculated rather to render inveterate in him a distaste for study, and a solid hatred of our craft.

Let us be less careful of the mere number of our classes, and more careful of their intellectual culture. Let us care more for what we think of ourselves, than what the public think of us. The respect of others follows close upon self respect. Let us not care to be called of men, *Rabbi, Rabbi.* Let us be content with classes of limited num-

bers, every member of which can keep pace
with a properly-advancing curriculum. Let
us aim at a broad and invigorating culture,
not a narrow and pedantic one; let us ig-
nore examinations of College or Civil service, and aim only at the great and searching examination of actual life. Let our aims
be high and generous, irrespective of the
exactions of unreasoning parents and well-
meaning but unqualified intermeddlers;
let our means of coercion be dignified, in
spite of the trials to which our tempers may
be exposed. Let us endeavor to make our
pupils love their work without fearing us.
They may live — God knows — to love *us*.
Whether they ever love us or not perhaps
matters but little, if we do our work single-
heartedly. The *mens conscia recti* is of itself
no mean reward. I am, perhaps, an enthu-
siast; but I have an idea, that, ere a generation is passed away, the last sound of the
last tawse will be heard in the leading gram-
mar-schools of Scotland. Her scholars will
be none the worse taught, and her schoolmasters none the less respected, when instruction has been made less rugged in her

aspect, and discipline is maintained by the more than hydraulic pressure of a persistent and continuous gentleness.

And, O brother schoolmaster, remember evermore the exceeding dignity of our calling. It is not the holiest of all callings; but it runs near and parallel to the holiest. The lawyer's wits are sharpened, and his moral sense not seldom blunted, by a life-long familiarity with ignorance, chicanery, and crime. The physician, in the exercise of a more beneficent craft, is saddened continually by the spectacle of human weakness and human pain. We have usually to deal with fresh and unpolluted natures. A noble calling, but a perilous. We are dressers in a moral and mental vineyard. We are undershepherds of the Lord's little ones; and our business it is to lead them into green pastures, by the sides of refreshing streams. Let us into our linguistic lessons introduce cunningly and imperceptibly all kinds of amusing stories; stories of the real kings of earth, that have reigned in secret, crownless and unsceptred; leaving the vain show of power to gilded toy-kings and make-believe statesmen; of the Angels that have walked the earth in the guise of holy men and holier women; of the Seraph-singers, whose music will be echoing for ever; of the Cherubim of power, that with the mighty wind of conviction and enthusiasm have winnowed the air of pestilence and superstition.

Yes, Friend, throw a higher poetry than all this into your linguistic work; the poetry of pure and holy motive. Then, in the coming days, when you are fast asleep under the green grass, they will not speak lightly of you over their fruit and wine, mimicking your accent, and retailing dull, insipid boy-pleasantries. Enlightened by the experience of fatherhood, they will see with a clear remembrance your firmness in dealing with their moral faults, your patience in dealing with their intellectual weakness. And, calling to mind the old schoolroom, they will think: "Ah! it was good for us to be there. For, unknown to us, were made therein three tabernacles; one for us, and one for our schoolmaster, and one for Him that is the Friend of all

children, and the Master of all schoolmasters."

Ah! believe me, brother mine, where two
or three children are met together, unless
He, who is the Spirit of gentleness, be in
the midst of them, then our Latin is but
sounding brass, and our Greek a tinkling
cymbal.

.

XXV.

SCHOLA IN NUBIBUS.

A LEARNED botanist informs us that no
flower is perfect. I am sorry to think he
should be able to prove so saddening an
assertion. What a world is this of ours, in
which our very symbols of purity are impure; of perfection, imperfect! Will chemistry detect a flaw in elemental diamond?

Poor Eve, as she went weeping out of
Eden, plucked a last nosegay; but every
flower she touched became infected with a
petal-plague; and the malady has gone
spreading through all the vegetable kingdom from that sad day to this. Each plant
has now its special part a-wanting. No
leafy thing can jeer at its green brother.
All come short of the perfect type of plant-
hood. A specimen, complete in all its parts,
may be sketched on paper to serve as a

criterion of the special deficiencies of particulars; but a perfect plant or a perfect
flower can no more be found in Nature,
than in the world a man utterly unselfish,
or a woman utterly devoid of goodness.

Naturalists give an account equally humiliating of the existing animal creation.
There appears to have been a physical Fall
of man and beast. It must have been a
curious sort of Zoological Garden where all
were corporeally perfect. But how strange
it is that all living creatures, biped or quad-
ruped, should be foxes that have lost their
tails? Why should we upbraid the mole
with blindness, or the sloth with inactivity?
A cat may point derisively to our now un-
flexile ears; a marmoset to our now unpre-
hensile toes; a baboon may grin at our
miserably poor, unswingable suggestions
of abortive tails.

Man then appears to have had two Falls;
or, perhaps, more correctly speaking, a
spiritual Fall, and a physical Rise. There
is an ebb and flow in everything. Nature
is for ever playing a simple, a monotonous,
but a terrible game. Odd and even, Heads

and Tails. See-saw, Marjory Daw. Here we
go up, up, up ; and here we go down, down,
down. If on the street a silver coin I find,
Forthwith my elbow through a window
goes: If Fortune on my right smile sweet
and kind, Fate on the left comes treading
on my toes. And so divines inform us
that spiritually we have been degenerat-
ing for six thousand years ; and naturalists
comfort us with the assurance that we have
the while been physically improving. On
the whole, then, we have been losers. By
the time we are as bad as Beelzebub, we
shall be as beautiful as Apollo. And Beelzebub and Apollo are philologically one.
—What a wonderful study is Philology !

It was after indulging in a train of some
such desultory reflections, and observing
the necessity of demonstrating actual im-
perfections by reference to a non-existent
type, that I was led, about the middle of
the next century, — in the spirit, or the
clouds of my tobacco-pipe,—to pay a visit
to an *olim* friend, whose name is carved by
the side of my own on the upper bench of
Old St. Edwards.

He now held a subordinate mastership in a public school, that was pleasantly situated at the foot of the Grampians. The buildings were stately, and the grounds charming. The playground commanded a not very distant view of noble, rugged mountains: and a short walk brought you to the banks of a romantic trouting-stream. The pupils were some hundred and fifty in number and belonged chiefly to the class of gentry, or to the upper middle-class of society. The staff of masters was selected from the most distinguished scholars and mathematicians of our Universities; and the curriculum of study included English, French, Italian, German, Latin, Greek, and Mathematics. The latter branch extended over Euclid, Algebra, Trigonometry, and the Conic Sections. The pupils entered usually at the age of nine, and remained for a term of seven years. A few, who were destined for the learned professions, stayed sometimes for an extra year, or even longer, by way of preparation for the highest honors of our Universities.

The Principal of the place was a Clergyman or Minister: the religious and moral training of the boys was under his sole charge. Consequently on Sundays he was undisputed master of all arrangements; and on week-days he presided in chapel, morning and evening. His tuition was confined to Biblical and Profane History, in which subjects he delivered two prelections daily to the classes in turn, in such a way that each class attended one Biblical prelection, and two prelections on Profane History, every week. His classes were the favorite ones, I was told; and no wonder; for the Principal had learning and tact sufficient to make his lectures wonderfully interesting, and the sacredness of his calling exempted him from the necessity of employing punishment of any kind as a stimulant or preventive.

The pupils of the first year were engaged in the close and analytic study of their own language, and in Writing and Arithmetic. French was taught them upon a conversational rather than a philological or grammatical method. During the second year Italian was thrown in on the same method, and continued with the former studies to the close of the session.

The third year commenced with Latin, and this with the previous branches carried the pupils to the end of their fourth year.

German was now introduced; but the modern tongues were taught almost entirely as spoken languages; and, as no very extensive preparation was required for them out of class, these studies did not weigh very heavily upon the young pupils. Latin was commenced upon the *vivâ voce* principle, but became gradually more and more analytic, and was made the chief instrument for inculcating the philosophy of language. As every Classical Master was more or less conversant with the modern tongues, ample use was made of the idioms of these latter in illustrating the idioms of an ancient language.

At the commencement of the sixth year a select few, generally boys of superior talents, began the study of Greek; and from their previous linguistic training it was marvellous with what rapidity they progressed in the study of this intricate tongue.

For a time the *vivâ voce* method was adhered to, and it was really refreshing to hear the natural music of the spoken Greek. The other pupils, who were not intended for the learned professions, continued their former studies, which carried them gradually into wide and interesting fields of History, Oratory, Poetry, and Philosophy.

The plan of study, here drawn out, was not rigidly adhered to in all cases. There were several pupils, who, from reasons of health or comparative mental deficiency, were allowed to drop one or more of the Modern languages; and some, after a while, were exempted from the study of Latin.

The study of Geometry was commenced in the fourth year; but, after a fair trial, pupils were sent back to practical arithmetic who evinced no capacity for abstract mathematical studies; and those who showed a marked and special turn for the latter were allowed exemptions from many other branches, to admit of their giving full attention to their favorite pursuits. Indeed, there were one or two instances of senior pupils, of about eighteen years of age, who had stayed beyond the usual term, and were engaged in the study of the Calculi.

I was especially pleased with the chapel service on Sundays, which was judiciously short and reasonably long. The singing of the hymns and anthems was exquisite. I was informed that, with the exception of a few boys who were physically unable to whistle a tune, the pupils generally could read simple music with ease; and that several of them could play on one or two musical instruments with considerable effect. A concert was given at the close of my visit, and at my special request, in the great hall; where several glees and madrigals were admirably sung, in some of which one of the masters took a prominent part; and a quartette was played more than passably by three of the pupils and the same master, who was an excellent player, it appeared, on the pianoforte and organ.

I must confess, I was a little amused to find that even dancing was not entirely lost sight of; but the lessons in this department were entirely optional.

The Principal and all the masters breakfasted and dined with the boys in the great hall; and once a month the dinner-table was honored with the presence of their wives, and lady-visitors from the neighborhood. These days were, of course, *cretati;* and every one was bound to appear in his best clothes and his best manners; and very often on these occasions the evening was spent in music or theatricals, or both, in the great hall.

I went round the dormitories, and found that each boy had a *separate*, well-ventilated room. On the table of each room was a New Testament; but whether it was much read in each instance, I am of course unable to state; at all events, if it was ever read in any one instance, it would be read *spontaneously*, and not from the motives of either fear or hypocrisy.

The Sunday arrangements struck me as being remarkable for the extreme, and, to my mind, excessive liberality they evinced in the Principal, who was, as I have stated, a minister of the gospel. The boys attended service twice; once in the morning and once in the evening. In the afternoon they

were allowed to walk in the grounds; under
the cloisters in wet weather; or to read
quietly in the public library.   There was a
considerable range of book-shelves from
which books might be selected; and these
books were by no means confined to religious subjects. I was, although a layman,
startled, and indeed a little shocked, to find
that the Principal had not excluded from
the Sunday shelves many books of profane
travels, and many of the works of Johnson,
Goldsmith, Washington Irving, and a terrible phalanx of secular poets, such as Cow-
per, Gray, Southey, Wordsworth, and Tennyson. However, as the reverend Principal
was a man of undoubted piety, of very extensive learning, and capable of defending
his views with sound logic and good-hu-
mored banter, I kept my opinions to myself;
but I resolved in my own mind, that if ever
I sent a son or nephew to this school, I
should previously stipulate that on Sundays
his readings should be confined entirely to
useful sermons and entertaining tracts.

I was so charmed with all I saw in my
short visit to this beautiful valley, that at

times I thought I was enacting the part of Rasselas. One morning, however, in my rambles I stumbled, in a sequestered place, upon a knot of little fellows who were in a great state of excitement, and somewhat annoyed, apparently, at my fortuitous interference. In a moment I perceived the cause of the meeting. There had been a fight. One little fellow was being led away, victorious, with a bloody nose; and another, with a black eye, was being comforted under defeat. I was at once bound over to secrecy. However, the combat was discovered, all through the unfortunate black eye, that very evening by the Principal, who certainly did not visit the matter very severely upon the chief delinquents. "The fact is," said he to me in private, "the boys were pretty much of a size, and there was a little bad blood between them, which this fight has let in a wholesome way. I gave them an imposition, and some words of kindly counsel; but really, in my heart, I was not very angry; for they are both capital lads, and will now be the fastest of friends." In the case of bullying, however, I was told that the Principal was exceedingly severe. One case of a very aggravated description had come before him two years previously, and he had had recourse to a singular mode of jury-trial. A council was held of all the Masters and the Captain of each year: the vote of each individual, man or boy, being of one value. The Principal, who had no vote, stated the case fully, and the culprit was allowed to make his defence in words or in writing, personally or by proxy. In this instance the culprit was expelled, although one vote in four would have exempted him from that extreme penalty.

I was particularly struck with one feature of this Institution. I was speaking to the Principal of the open Scholarships, and Medals, and Fellowships at our great Universities, and the prizes in the various departments of our Civil Service that had been thrown open to public competition; and I inquired if any special arrangements were meant to qualify—I meant *cram*, but I was afraid to use the word — to qualify pupils for those special ends. The Principal answered me half-gravely, half-smilingly :

" When I preach to my little fellows on
Sundays, or lecture to them on week-days,
I endeavor continually to bring before
them the example of One, who went about
doing good, simply because goodness was
good. And from early and later Christian
history, and from profane history as well, I
can show them instances of men, who
throughout laborious lives preferred virtue
to profit, goodness to glitter. To my colleagues is entrusted the intellectual education of my charges. They would be
counteracting much of my teaching, if they
were continually to be placing before their
pupils sordid motives of gain, or even the
less ignoble but still unholy motives of ambition. I should prefer a boy to be led on
to work, merely because work was his duty;
and I should wish a teacher to do his ut-
most to make that duty a pleasure. It is
the business of my colleagues to give a
general and broad intellectual training to
their pupils, that the latter may be fitted,
some for professional life hereafter, and all
for the position of gentlemen : should prizes
fall in their way, they will be welcome,

although they were never our special ends
in view. My duty is to prepare my boys,
by my poor teaching and my poorer example,
for the fulfilment in after life of simple social and Christian duties. There is only
one prize for which my teaching prepares
boys or men: it is a very high prize, and
very hard in the gaining. And whether or
no that prize is ever gained, I am unable to
tell. For I stand upon my little Pisgah, and
am forbidden to follow in haste. I can only
state this for my colleagues and myself,
that, while we should be glad enough to hear
of particular instances where brilliant success at our Universities or in the busy world
were attained by our pupils, we should be
far more thankful to find that they were
generally esteemed in after life as intelligent gentlemen and good Christians."

Towards the close of my visit, I was present one afternoon in the private library of
the Principal, when a small *posse* of senior
pupils came to bid him farewell before
leaving for the University. After a long
and pleasant and familiar conversation, the
Principal rose, and, standing in front of the

fireplace, addressed his small but attentive
audience to the following effect. As I
write from memory, I give the purport only
of his words.

"I am now addressing you, Boys, for the
last time *ex catherdrâ*. Listen then to a few
words of advice, and give them hereafter
some little heed. On entering the University, do not follow the received dogma, that
a Freshman is traditionally bound to ex-
travagance or folly. Be in no hurry to form
acquaintances. Sympathetic friendships
will cluster round you in due time. Associate, by preference, with those of your own
rank, or with those a little above it. Neither
seek nor avoid the company of the very
exalted; but never associate with men
beneath you in social position, however
wealthy, affable, or good tempered they
may be. Of course, if a man be possessed
of surpassing abilities or unusual force of
character, in his case social distinctions
are annihilated.

"Read with a view to Final Honors only,
without swerving aside to win special prizes
or scholarships. Should these latter fall

naturally in your way, you can try for them without harm. In the perusal of classic authors observe closely all mannerisms, and imitate none; though to do so would give you extra marks in an Examination. In translating an ancient writer never strain an idiom of your own tongue for the purpose of showing the accuracy of your scholarship. The idea is incorrect that pure scholarship of necessity entails a corruption of native taste. The idea was at one time generally entertained; and has now, I regret to state, many learned supporters, whose hybrid English should be a warning to young scholars.

"In your College lecture-room listen with respectful attention to what is said; but abstain from taking notes. Half of what you hear were better forgotten; with much of the remainder you will probably disagree: what residue is worth remembering will be remembered for its singularity.

"Your chronology is more favorable than my own. There are three public Professors now at Oxford, whose catholic and unpedantic lectures are replete with

interest and instruction; their united efforts
have thrown a new vitality into the old dry
Academic teaching. Cambridge can boast
of no genial and wise philosopher that can
render the study of Greek a study of more
than verbal subtlety, like the Friend of
youth at Balliol: no Cantab Latinist can
compete in combined learning and usefulness with Mr. Conington; though a parallel
to Mr. Arnold in poetry and enthusiasm
may be found in a Cambridge Professor of
History. This superiority of Oxford in professorial teaching would weigh more heavily
with me than even her present, but I trust
only temporary, superiority in boat-racing.
Had I ten sons, I should send them all to
Oxford, under present circumstances. At
Trinity, Cambridge, an advanced student
may now attend not without profit a classical lecture room. In my own day, at this
latter University, such a student might attend for a year the classical lectures of a College Tutor or an University Professor without one sentence falling from the lips of
either that was worth picking up, except
for the purpose of throwing out of window.

" Use a Dictionary as seldom as possible, a Grammar, never; an annotated edition of a classic only where an author does not explain himself by himself, or is not illustrated by cotemporary writers. I would caution you in particular against the study of German writings on classical subjects. In the notes of Porson and Elmsley you taste the pure and delicate aroma of classical learning: in the exhaustive Excursuses of Hermann and Heyne you have the fibre boiled down with the leaf: in modern English critics you have the over-boiled mixture of the Germans *re-boiled*. The longevity of the patriarchal days is passed for ever; otherwise, a hoary youth might amuse his fiftieth decennium with plodding through the learned volumes that have very nearly made Horace dull.

" Continue your reading of modern languages, as a wholesome alterative in the midst of classical and scientific studies. Do not avoid the society of ladies. To pass an evening with a high-bred, accomplished, and intellectual Lady is for mental improvement equivalent to the perusal of two books

of the Æneid, or of one Greek Play. Travel
abroad when you have the opportunity:
obtain what introductions you can to foreign
men of letters; seek admission to the stu-
dios of Artists, and the rooms of Musicians;
and perfect your accent of each tongue in
these best of all schools, not neglecting the
Café and the Theatre.

" In dress follow fashion at a short distance, so as never to be quite in it, or quite
out of it. In everything avoid singularity.
Guard against prejudices or superstitions
of College and University. There is more
wisdom without the walls of either than
within them. Let there be nothing about
you to designate your School, College, University, nationality, or religious denomina-
tion.

" Never mention my name except in answer to a question; and in your festive
meetings forget me altogether. An eulogy
spoken on such occasions is tedious to the
hearer, and no compliment to the subject.

" Be slow in forming your opinion of
others; and slower in expressing it. Use a
superlative word as seldom as possible in

conversation. In speech or writing aim at perspicuity rather than at wit. He who speaks to be understood is thinking of his hearer; he who studies his expressions is thinking of himself; and a brilliant talker is seldom a polite one. Never attempt an epigram in conversation, until you have seen more of men and manners. The epigrammatic sharpness of a young man is but the condensation of sciolism. Oracular brevity is the prerogative of age and experience.

"Never canvass your own characters, even in confidential converse with an intimate friend. He who touches on a good quality of his own is weakening what he touches. But while self-praise enfeebles, self-disparagement emasculates. Repentance of the heart is silent, even in the recesses of the closet: it is subtler than any gas or ether, and is sure to escape through open lips, or to evaporate in words. Besides, he who bemoans a weakness to a neighbor is too often preparing himself to give way to it, and repenting by anticipation.

"If you are in any temporary distress, pecuniary or otherwise, apply frankly to

your fathers or to myself. If in spiritual
trouble, I would gladly give you help, if
help were in my power to give ; but I would
counsel you to seek help from the Father
of us all, and from Him alone.

" Respect authority, but never fear it;
and respect yourselves more than all authority. Be chivalrous to all women of all ranks
for the sake of your mothers or their memories. Be religious in such a way that no
one may suspect you of being so, or take a
liberty with sacred subjects in your presence as though you were the opposite."

It was with most unaffected regret that I
bade good-bye at last to my friend, his
colleagues, and their admirable Principal.
I confess I do not even yet fully understand the character of the latter. For, while
there are phases in it that seem half-apos-
tolic, there are other phases that bespeak
the man of the world. At my departure,
with a smile he presented me with a cigar-
case filled with choice cigars; which circumstance I considered, and consider still,
as remarkably eccentric on his part; for,
although I smoked occasionally of an even-

ing in his library, I know for certain that *he* has not smoked a cigar for years.

And so, Reader, ended, as it began, my pleasant visit to the *Schola in Nubibus;* appropriately; in smoke.   Which thing is an allegory.